THE HUMANIST

by

WERoberts

Author's Note

Believe it or not, the idea for this story came to me one night in an amazingly detailed dream, and in the following days and weeks I strove to set it down much as I remembered it, making embellishments and additions as necessary. I realize that the finished work is flawed and rather heavily biased, and if I manage to offend or upset any of my readers with the ideas expressed in it I am wholeheartedly sorry. Of course, I know that there are many millions of religious believers in our world who are personifications of kindness and compassion, of fair-mindedness and tolerance; but sadly there are many others whose narrowness of perspective, sectarian bigotry and false sense of superiority over perceived 'heretical' outsiders have, through their actions, turned our world into a mire of violent confrontation, hatred and fear. It is for that reason that I believe this story deserves to be told, even with its faults.

I have set the story in Shelter Cove, California, because as a young man I visited the place two or three times and was deeply impressed by its physical isolation and the rugged natural beauty of its setting. But the name, location and general description of the town are the only things I have taken that are genuine – all other depictions of particular people and places, as well as any description of the general beliefs and character of the inhabitants, being completely fictional. I certainly do not intend to malign the town in any way with the negative qualities described in my story, which are entirely my own creation. Shelter Cove was, and I'm sure still remains, secluded and majestic, welcoming and friendly – a true jewel of the Lost California Coast.

WERoberts
April, 2015

1.

It was 3 PM that Friday when the phone rang and destroyed my weekend.

I was clearing my desk and loading my briefcase to escape, and had been looking forward to a quiet Saturday afternoon on my own at the apartment, watching a Giants game on the TV and chilling out with a few beers, but as soon as I heard my boss's voice I knew that that was never going to happen. When he calls me this late on a Friday there's always a good reason, and one that's almost certain to tie me up for the entire weekend.

'Arnold, can you step into my office, please?' he asked me. 'Bring a couple of lattes with you, okay?'

The lattes meant the interview was going to be serious. Now I definitely knew my relaxing weekend was toast.

'Sure thing, Abe,' I told him.

Five minutes later I knocked on the door of his glassed-in cubicle at the end of the newsroom and he waved me inside.

Abe Rawlings cultivates his image as a newspaper editor with care. Today he sat at his desk wearing a pale blue shirt with the cuffs rolled up to his elbows. His dark grey suit jacket was hanging from the coat rack in the corner, but he still wore the buttoned waistcoat. He looked the picture of the '40s Hollywood newshound – all that was missing was the green eye shade and the sleeve garters.

1

'Latte with brown sugar, right?' I said, depositing it on the desk before him.

'You remembered,' he said, reaching for it.

I lowered myself into the chair opposite him with my coffee, sat back and crossed my legs.

'So, what's up?'

He took a sip and settled back in his swiveling armchair, his face sobering.

'You're alone this weekend, right? Lisa's gone back to her mother?'

My sixteen year old daughter had been staying with me for the previous three weeks.

'Yep, I'm alone again. Put her on the plane last night. Now she's back with Momsy.'

'Good.'

'Why good?'

'Because I want you to do something for me.'

'I'm listening.'

Abe sat his latte on the desktop and lifted a few sheets of printout, then settled back in his chair again, leafing through them.

'A rather sad thing happened a couple days ago, Arnold. My nephew died.'

I shifted in my chair.

'Sorry to hear that. Were you close to him?'

'Not particularly, but I liked him. His name was Leo. Leo Walensky. He was my youngest sister's son. A very intelligent, sensitive young man. Seventeen years old. Apparently he fell from a cliff onto some rocks by the sea.'

'Not a nice way to go.'

'No, it isn't.' Abe laid the papers on his lap and looked over at me. 'But there's some question as to the manner in which he died, and if you don't mind I'd like you to go up there and check it out for me.'

I sat up.

'You think there might have been foul play involved?'

'I don't think anything yet, Arnold. It's too early for that. The police think it was either an accident or suicide, but that doesn't scan for me.'

Dropping the pages on the desk, Abe got up and turned to stand before the large window, looking out at the bay, his hands in his pockets.

'My sister Muriel lives with her dentist husband in a town called Shelter Cove, sixty to eighty miles south of Eureka in a stretch called the Lost California Coast.' He looked back at me. 'You been up that way yet, Arnold?'

I shook my head.

'Nice country.' He turned back to enjoy the view. 'Anyway, two days ago she called to give me the sad news. Apparently she and her husband and daughter had gone off for some afternoon shopping followed by dinner and a movie in Fortuna, the nearest big town. When they got home it was late so they just went to bed. They assumed Leo was fast asleep in his room, but when he didn't come down for breakfast the next morning they went looking for him. They found his bedroom empty and the bed still made. They tried getting him on his cell phone, but it had apparently been switched off. When they discovered that his bike was also gone they contacted the county sheriff's office and reported him missing. Three hours later the boy's body was found sprawled across some jagged rocks at the foot of a cliff.' Abe turned back towards me. 'I looked up the report of Leo's death on the local paper's website, the *Humboldt Times*, out of Eureka. I've got it here.'

He handed the printout pages across to me and stepped back, watching me with his arms folded while I looked them over. At the top of the article was a school photograph of a young man with long but well-groomed light-colored hair. Not a bad looking boy from what I could see – though he was wearing thickish tinted glasses, almost thick enough to be called 'bottle' glasses. Poor kid must have taken a lot of ribbing about that over the years.

I scanned the article beneath. It seemed a straightforward account of an all too common tragedy, quoting the Sheriff's Department as saying that the boy's death was apparently either an unfortunate accident or a suicide. In any case they were not looking for anyone else in connection with it.

'This account seems clear enough,' I told him. 'What do you think's wrong with it?'

Abe shook his head, frowning.

'I don't know. Maybe there's nothing there, but after spending forty plus years in this business I've got a nose for these things. Leo was a bright kid with a great future ahead of him. My sister said he was looking forward to leaving Shelter Cove in a few days for university. There was no indication he was depressed for any reason. On the contrary, she said he seemed happier than she'd seen him for some time.'

'Right. Well, that gets rid of the suicide scenario – unless there's something nobody knows about. What about the simple accident idea?'

Abe shook his head.

'The boy had lived in that town all his life, knew the local cliffs like the back of his hand. Wasn't any reason he should suddenly, on a clear sunny day, climb over a safety railing and fall to his death.'

'Those things happen, Abe.'

'Yeah, they do. But there's something else – something that puts the whole event in a different light.' He stood before the window and stared at me, his hands now in his pockets again. 'This morning I called up the man who found him, the local law up there in Shelter Cove – a Humboldt County Sheriff's deputy named Horace Williams. He was still pretty shocked from finding the body and let slip a couple of things that got me thinking.'

'What kind of things?'

'Well, for one, Leo had apparently become a bit of an outcast in the town over the last few months. It seems he harbored some rather unusual beliefs and made no bones about letting people know about them. My sister made no mention of that to me, but from what I gathered from the deputy a lot of the town fathers disapproved mightily of Leo's activities. Some might even be pleased that he's gone.'

'Interesting. What were these "beliefs"?'

Abe sat down in his chair again, took a sip of his coffee.

'He wouldn't say. But they must have been pretty wild to have created such negative feelings in the town. I'd call Muriel and ask her about it, but she's already going through enough hell without me pressuring her for more information. The funeral's next Thursday and I'll certainly be going up for that, but in the meantime I think it's best I just leave them alone.'

'Do they think there's anything suspicious about their son's death?' I asked him.

He sat back in his chair.

'They don't believe he killed himself, that's for sure. As far as the accident angle is concerned, Muriel couldn't say either way. It might have been an accident, but he was usually a very careful kid, didn't take stupid risks.' He took another sip of coffee, put the cup down and looked up at me again. 'Anyway, I want you to take a drive up there tomorrow, Arnold. Spend a few days, see what you can dig up. It might be nothing. On the other hand it might turn out to be something that involves the whole damned community in some kind of a criminal cover-up. And if there's a story, I want you to find it.'

I drained my latte and stood up.

'Sure, Abe, I'll drive up there if you want me to. On the face of it, though, while your nephew's death is certainly a sad event, the details as I understand them so far don't seem that suspicious to me.'

Abe lifted his index finger.

'There's one other thing.'

'Yeah?'

'Leo was visually challenged. He suffered from a condition known as aniridia, which means he was born without irises. He couldn't see well enough to drive, that's why he rode his bike all the time. He also had to wear glasses, partly to improve his limited vision and partly, when outdoors, to block out the bright sunlight. Three days ago it was clear and sunny up there, and even in the late afternoon he'd have had to wear his outdoor dark glasses.'

'So?'

'When the body was found he wasn't wearing them.'

'They were probably dislodged when he fell over the cliff.'

'Uh-uh. Couldn't have been. When he rode his bicycle Leo always wore an elastic strap around his head that held the glasses in place, so they wouldn't be jarred off when he hit potholes.'

'They could still have fallen off.'

'Nope.'

'How can you be so sure?'

'Deputy Williams said that when he did a close search of the rough ground around the vista point parking area he found the glasses off to one side behind a rock. Said it looked almost as if they'd been tossed there.'

For a long moment I just stood by my chair looking back at Abe, running the bits of his story through my mind. Then I settled back onto the seat, sat the latte cup on the desk and pulled out my notepad.

'Okay,' I told him. 'I guess you'd better fill me in on everything you know about it if I'm going up there.'

Abe did.

Fifteen minutes later I collected my laptop and briefcase from my desk, scooped up my brown leather jacket off the chair back, and set off for home to prepare for the journey.

It might seem strange to some that a local paper like the *South Bay Bulletin* could afford to send me two hundred miles up the coast to spend several days checking out a story that could at best be only of moderate interest to Bay area readers, but Abe Rawlings was fortunate enough to have founded his paper in a commuter town adjacent to a major west coast university, so there were thousands of well-educated, discerning residents on hand who were tired of the big time syndicated approach to news reporting of the *Examiner* and the *Chronicle*, and who were proud supporters of the *Bulletin*'s record of feisty but solid investigative journalism – with past exposés to its credit involving flagrant election fraud at the state capital and corruption in the San Francisco police force. So for Abe, who had cut his teeth at the news desk of the *Washington Post* under Ben Bradlee a score of years earlier, the usual limitations imposed on small town papers by a lack of newsworthy local material and/or reader indifference were not an issue, and he went after – or sent his reporters after (usually me, as I am single and currently unattached) – any story state-wide that his acute newsman's intuition told him might prove interesting. He was seldom wrong. What's more, Abe had married an obscenely wealthy San Francisco socialite widow, so that what the paper's coffers couldn't stump up for these long-distance investigative junkets Abe himself made up from his own pocket.

If on a good day you drive north out of San Francisco on Highway 101 as I did the following morning, passing over the Golden Gate Bridge and then on up through the North Bay and the Santa Rosa Plain past the cities of Cloverdale and Ukiah, you find yourself very quickly in some of the finest country to be seen in America. It was all new to me, rolling along with the driver's window open in my battered blue Chevy Cobalt with the warm wind blowing in my face. For a mid-westerner like myself, only recently transplanted to the west coast from the relative flatness (and dullness) of Des Moines, the unfolding buff-colored countryside that rolled past me that balmy late August morning, with its scrub oak-covered hills bounding broad valleys of lush green vineyards, was balm to my eyes and to my spirit – a welcome break from the overpopulated asphalt nightmare that is the urban sprawl of South Bay San Francisco.

But the country that really caught my attention came a couple of hours later when I reached Humboldt County and the section of the highway that paralleled the serpentine Eel River. For here are the forests of the *sequoia sempervirens*, the giant redwood trees that I'd been told about but had not yet seen for myself (an area also known, coincidentally, as the center of illegal marijuana-growing in the state). And after enjoying several miles of spectacular scenery – where occasionally the road would narrow to two lanes for a stretch to wind precariously between the massive trunks of the great trees, their thick high canopy shuttering down the sunlight to a shadowy, cathedral-like ambiance – I turned off four-lane 101 at Garberville to take the two-lane mountain highway that led west towards the coast. The quiet community of Shelter Cove is situated at the end of this twisting twenty-three mile road on a point of land projecting into the wild sea surges of one of the roughest and rockiest sections of California's notoriously beautiful northern coastline. Indeed the phrase that came continually to mind as I rolled past the rippling creeks and through the thick groves of redwood and fir, gazing up in wonder at the rugged corrugations of the King Range through which I was winding, was that this scenery warranted that old corker of a description 'God's country'. For patently this was God's country, and even though I didn't believe in that Divine Entity myself, in this instance I was in wholehearted accord with the sentiment.

Breaking out at long last onto the tableland overlooking the sea, where the small town of Shelter Cove sprawled beneath random copses of wind-twisted pine and fir trees, I was pleased to note that my destination was in no way an anticlimax after the pleasures I had enjoyed on the drive. A collection of a few hundred dwellings and commercial buildings, with a small bay at its southern edge providing shelter for a dozen or so fishermen's boats, Shelter Cove also sported, at its center, a short but adequate airstrip to accommodate the light planes of those residents and visitors who could afford to commute to and from civilization that way. At first sight the town was neat, smartly maintained and pleasantly laid out, and I was pleased that my assignment would keep me there, more than likely, for some days.

After cruising the main streets for a few minutes to get a feel of the place I turned off at 'The Tides', a modest-looking motel beside the seafront that was the first I had seen with a 'Vacancy' sign lit up. I pulled up before the office, shut down and went inside. Behind the counter an older man in a checked flannel shirt leafed through a local newspaper. Above his head a wall clock told me it had just turned 1 PM. The man glanced up at me with a half smile as I came through the door.

'Afternoon,' he said.

'Good afternoon. You got a non-smoking room I could have for a few days?'

The man reached for a ledger on a desk behind him, opened it, and produced a ballpoint pen from his shirt pocket.

'A few days, huh? Well, you're lucky. We've had a cancellation. I think we can fix you up all right.'

He checked the ledger, then turned and plucked a key from a wall rack.

'Number 21, down at the end. Want to take a look?'

'No, I'm sure it's fine.'

He swung the ledger around and pointed and while he swiped my card I entered my name and the car license number. Then I signed where required and he handed my card back with the door key.

'Let me know if you need anything.'

'Thanks, I will.' I started for the door.

'You here to fish?'

I turned back to him. 'Maybe. Can you recommend a good restaurant in Shelter Cove?'

He scratched his head.

'Well, there're three or four good places, but if you want the best I'd go to the Cove down near the jetty. Great seafood. Good steaks, too.'

'Thanks for that. I'll give it a try.'

The room was light, clean and spacious, with a back window opened to allow the sea breeze to freshen the air. Beside the bed was the phone and – unusually – a black Bible with a card resting on it detailing the service schedule for the local Episcopalian Church and inviting visitors to drop in. Of course I'd seen many Gideon Bibles in motel drawers in my time, but never before a proper Bible laid out in the open. Clearly someone was eager to spread the word. I slipped the Bible into the drawer and headed off for a wash.

Forty minutes later I was in the Cove Restaurant, seated at a booth overlooking the sea, having just consumed a decently made club sandwich. On the table before me was a nearly empty coffee cup and my open notepad.

I'd been trying to organize the little information I had about Leo Walensky's death, and making a list of people I'd better see here in Shelter Cove. Of course, sooner or later I would have to speak with Abe's sister Muriel and her husband, but I wasn't ready for that yet. I thought it best to leave them alone to grieve for a while and to glean what facts I could from the surrounding community first before bothering that poor family with my questions.

'More coffee?'

The Cove waitress was at my elbow, holding a coffeepot.

'Sure. Thanks.'

She bent over to fill my cup. When she did so I got a whiff of her perfume. Very pleasant; a cut above what one usually got with waitresses. Chanel? I couldn't be sure. A lady in her mid-thirties, she was wearing a dark knee-length skirt and a white peasant blouse with short puffy sleeves and a deep elasticized front that showed the curvature of her full breasts. It was a nice view; she was a good looking woman. She stood back and smiled down at me.

'You here on business?'

'You could say that.'

'What's your line?'

I sat back in my seat.

'Reporter for a Bay area paper.' Her eyebrows went up but other than that she made no response. There was a nametag pinned over her left breast. 'Can you spare me a minute, Lorraine? Got a couple questions for you, if you wouldn't mind.'

She glanced off towards the main part of the restaurant where two booths were occupied by couples eating their lunches. Then she sat down on the banquette opposite, setting the coffeepot on the Formica tabletop between us.

'Sure. I can give you a couple minutes. Fire away.'

I smiled and took a sip from my refilled cup.

'Thanks. I'm Arnie, by the way. Arnie Rednapp.' I reached across to shake her hand and we exchanged smiles. Then I sat back again and my smile faded. 'Sad business, the death of that boy, wasn't it?'

Her face was impassive.

'The Walensky boy? Sure was. Always sad when somebody young goes.' She cocked her head to one side. 'Is that why you're here?'

I moved my mouth.

'Maybe.'

She looked curious.

'Now why should such a thing – tragic as it is – catch the attention of someone from so far away?'

I shrugged.

'Human interest. As you said, it's always sad when a young person dies.' I took another sip. 'Did you know the boy?'

'No. Oh, I've seen him around now and then, riding his bike. But he never came in here. Seemed just an ordinary kid to me.'

I leaned forward.

'Are you from Shelter Cove, Lorraine?'

'Me? Oh, no. I've been here only three years. Came up here from L.A. after my divorce was finalized.'

'Got any kids?'

'A daughter.' She cocked her head again. 'Why do you ask?'

'Your daughter must have known the Walensky boy.'

'Oh, no. Mandy's only twelve. The Walensky boy just graduated from high school.'

'Ah. Where is the high school? Here in Shelter Cove?'

'No. Kids that age get a bus every day that takes them over the mountains to Fortuna. Up to the eighth grade they go to the cream colored school up the road.'

I nodded.

'Did you ever hear anything about the boy? Any rumors being kicked around about him amongst the local population?'

She frowned slightly.

'Why should I hear such things?'

'Well, you're a waitress. You hover around tables and counters filling coffee cups.'

'I don't eavesdrop.'

'I'm sure you don't. But you might hear something just the same.'

'Well, I've never heard anything about that boy in any case. Sorry.'

'Okay.' I took another sip of coffee. 'What kind of a town is Shelter Cove, Lorraine? Can you describe it to me?'

She glanced again towards the front of the restaurant, ran her hand around the back of her hair.

'Well,' she said, laughing nervously, 'It's just like any other town, really. A larger percentage of older families, maybe. A fair number of wealthy people – now. It started out as a logging and fishing community back in the old days, but since the mills closed down there's not been much here to keep people going – except for the fishing, and tourism. Quite a lot of the laid-off workers moved on to find work elsewhere and their places were bought up by property developers. As

12

you can see, they tore down the old and built new – turned the town into a haven for retirees, and built summer homes for the city people from down south who come up here at the weekends and during the holidays for the sport fishing and the quiet. But basically it's just like everywhere else.'

I nodded.

'How would you describe the population of the town as a whole? Are they liberal or conservative in their outlook on things?'

She laughed.

'Well, they don't like environmentalists, that's for sure. At least the old residents who stayed don't. But the elected officials have been Democrat for as long as I've been here. I'd say most Shelter Cove residents are just good, hard-working God-fearing folk who mind their own business.'

I nodded and smiled again, moving my half-empty cup around with the tip of one finger.

'Who would you say were the real power people in the town, the ones who call the shots locally?'

She looked down, thinking.

'The mayor, I guess. Gus Willis. He's a realtor. Made a fortune in property development over the years. He comes in here sometimes. He's a friend of the boss.'

I made a note on my pad.

'Anybody else?'

'Reverend Baker of the Episcopalian Church. He's always at community meetings speaking out against one thing or another. Then there's Dale Anders. He's the P.E. teacher at Fortuna High School and coach of the football team. He's also my boss, owns this restaurant and motel, among other things. He has a lot to do with what goes on around here.'

Two more notes.

'That the lot?'

She smiled. 'Pretty much. Anything else?'

'No, not just now. Maybe later?'

I caught her eye and smiled back at her. She slid out of her seat and stood up, picking up the coffee pot.

'You in town for a few days, Arnie?'

'I might be.'

'Well, good,' she purred. 'I hope you enjoy your stay.'

'I'm sure I will.' She started off. 'Oh, Lorraine?' She turned, eyebrows lifted expectantly. 'Do you know where I can find Deputy Sheriff Horace Williams?'

She shook her head, disappointed.

'He stops by here a couple times a day for coffee. He was in here an hour ago. Back out on his rounds, I guess. You could try his home, but he's seldom there during shift hours. His wife, Edna, will be, though.'

She described how I could find the deputy's house, then left me to finish my coffee. When I did I left some money together with a handsome tip on the check and went out to my car.

Deputy Williams lived in a modest, ranch-style home on the side of a hill a couple miles inland. I pulled into his empty drive and got out. There was a small lawn edged with well-kept flowerbeds and rhododendron and azalea bushes. Inside the house a large dog barked as I approached. I rang the front bell and after a few moments the dog stopped and the door opened. Through the screen I could see a young woman holding a baby.

'Yes?'

'Mrs. Williams?'

'That's right.'

'I'm looking for your husband. Is he at home?'

'No, he's not. He's out on the road somewhere. I don't expect him back till five or five-thirty.'

I pulled a card from my wallet, scrawled my motel details on the back and handed it to her past the screen.

'I wonder if you could ask him to give me a call when he gets in? My cell number's on the card. I need to talk to him.'

'I'll tell him.'

'Thank you, Mrs. Williams. Have a good day.'

What to do now that was constructive? My watch told me it was now nearly 3 PM. I had a couple of hours to kill so I decided I'd try to find the spot where the boy had died, check it out for myself. For the next half hour I crawled the car around seafront roads in the town but could find nothing that looked like the secluded vista point of the newspaper's description. Then I remembered. As I had entered the town after winding through the King Range I had noticed a long building off to my left, The Shelter Cove General Store. Opposite it on my right had been a turning with a road sign that read 'Vista Point and Beach'. I drove back there and turned down that road. Three minutes later I came to a secluded parking area on a knoll overlooking the sea. The parking area was flanked on each side by a stand of coastal fir trees that blocked the town and pretty much everything else from sight. Not much traffic came out this way, certainly not in the late afternoon. I got out of the car and walked around to check out the view. It was spectacular. A steel railing about two feet high separated the parking lot from the eight or ten feet of rocky ground and bushes that defined the cliff edge. Carefully, I stepped over the fence, dropped to my hands and knees and inched forward to look over the edge. This was the place, surely. A hundred feet below frothy seawater crashed against sawtooth rocks at the base of the sheer wall of stone. It would have been an ugly way to go, that was clear.

Poor Leo.

Withdrawing from the edge, I rose, brushed off my pants, and climbed back over the railing. I started searching the area around the parking lot, looking for whatever I could find. There wasn't much to see. The spot was frequented enough so that the grass was pressed down and matted, and nothing looked out of the ordinary. I poked around a few minutes more, looking for the rock beside which the glasses had been discovered, but found nothing.

I was about to return to the car when a flash of white at the edge of my vision arrested me. A dozen yards away, at the side of the paved area, a crumpled ball of paper had become lodged in the branches of a low bush. I walked over, knelt down and extracted the paper, pulling it open as I stood up. It was a tract of some kind, headed by the title '*The Humanist*'. In one corner at the bottom of the page was a red smudge that could have been a bloody fingerprint. I quickly scanned the text – an intelligently written description of the basic tenets of humanist ideology, contrasted with a brief but telling argument against belief in God and the embracing of improvable dogma.

Over the years I had read some humanist authors myself – advocates of that revered tradition of open-minded questioning that began with the ancient Greeks, and whose ideas in more recent times have been defined in the writings of such highly regarded philosophers, literary figures and social commentators as Thomas Paine, Felix Adler, Kurt Vonnegut and Gore Vidal – so I knew the basics of their philosophy. What is primal in humanistic thought is the necessity of accepting personal responsibility for making decisions as to what makes behavior good or evil, right or wrong – making up one's own mind about questions regarding morality and ethics without relying upon the predeterminations of religious teachings. On the face of it – given the confrontational horrors of our era – this point of view has always seemed to me to deserve fair consideration by all people struggling to make sense of their lives. It was strange, however, to find such progressive ideas expounded in a handbill in the wilds of northern California.

The last couple of paragraphs on the page were a listing of graphically described recent massacres and atrocities carried out around the world by various fundamentalist religious groups. It made grim reading. The syntax was unpolished but clear – the work of a young mind, I reckoned, but one with exceptional intelligence and a fluent gift of expression. The tract was dated three days previously. I wondered what it was and who had written it? Why had it been left there, crumpled up and discarded?

Was the red smudge really blood, and if so, whose?

More importantly, did it have anything to do with Leo Walensky?

Without really knowing why, I folded the sheet and slipped it into the inside pocket of my jacket. Then I went back to my car.

It was time to await the deputy's call.

2.

The contact from Deputy Williams came at six o'clock, just as I was starting to watch the network news on the motel room's television – more graphic reports of atrocities committed by the various factions in Syria, another gory suicide bombing in Karachi. The usual depressing horrors. It wasn't my cell phone ringing that interrupted my viewing but a tap at the door. I killed the television with the remote and went to open it. Outside the young deputy stood holding my card.

'Mr. Rednapp?'

'That's right.'

'My wife said you wanted to see me.'

'I do. Please, come in.'

I stood back and opened the door wide. The deputy came in and stood uneasily by the window. I shut the door and gestured toward the single armchair beside him.

'Have a seat.'

'Thanks.' He did so, taking off his wide-brimmed hat and holding it in his lap. His crew-cut hair was carrot red. 'Now what's this all about? How can I help you?'

Moving to the far side of the double bed, I picked up my notepad and pen.

'The day before yesterday you received a call from my editor, Abe Rawlings of the *South Bay Bulletin*?'

'That's right. He wanted to know about the death of young Leo Walensky.'

'Uh-huh. And you were kind enough to give him a few details about the death, the discovery of the body, etc. Do you mind if I ask you a few more questions about it, Deputy Williams?'

'Not at all.'

I sat down on the foot of the bed with my notepad on my knee.

'You found the body the morning the boy was reported missing, right?'

'Correct. When I got the call from his folks I started poking around, talked to some of the local kids, asked if they'd seen him the previous afternoon. One of them had. He told me he'd seen Leo riding his bike out toward the vista point. So I went out there and had a look. It didn't take long to find his bike. Then, when I looked over the cliff edge, well ...'

He shook his head and shuddered.

'Mm. And how long did it take to recover the body?'

'About three hours. I had to contact the search and rescue people. They came out and abseiled down to collect it.'

'Did you stay at the scene the whole time?'

'Yessir. To keep any curious bystanders away.'

I made some notes.

'When the body was brought up, did you notice anything about the boy's injuries that wasn't consistent with what he would've suffered from the fall?'

The officer looked blank.

'I don't understand.'

'Is it possible that he'd sustained any injuries before his fall, like bruising or cuts?'

The deputy looked skeptical. 'You mean, like, if somebody had knocked him around a little beforehand?'

'That's right.'

Williams shook his head.

'No way of knowing, sir. His face was pretty banged up from being scraped on the rocks, never mind what happened in the fall itself. It wasn't a pretty sight, I can tell you.'

'I'm sure it wasn't.'

'Anyway, who would've beaten him up out there?'

I smiled across at him and let that lie, then checked my notes.

'Has there been an autopsy of the body, Deputy?'

'Sure. Standard procedure.'

'Can you tell me what was in the Coroner's report?'

He crossed his arms and sat back.

'Well, there were lacerations and bruises all over his body, and broken bones, too – including his back. But the blow that killed him was at the back of his head on the right side. Crushed his skull, it said. He would've died instantly.'

'I see. But you say his face was banged up, too?'

'That's right.'

I made a note.

'When you found the body, Deputy, how was it positioned on the rocks?'

Williams looked puzzled. 'What d'you mean?'

'Was the boy on his back, on his side, or face down on the rocks?'

'He was face down when I found him.'

'Mm. Then I wonder how it was he got the fatal blow on the back of his head?'

Williams smirked.

'The boy's body had been down there for over twelve hours, Mr Rednapp. There'd been at least one high tide in that time, maybe two. The rocks he was laying on aren't completely submerged during most high tides, but they are awash. His body probably got thrown around a lot down there in the surges and came to rest at last the way I found it.'

'Makes sense,' I said. I made another note. 'You told my editor that he wasn't wearing his glasses when he was found?'

'That's right. Not that they would have stayed on him down there in any case. But later on – I told your editor this – I found the glasses behind a rock at the side of the parking area.'

'Right.' I glanced up from my note taking. 'And you found nothing suspicious in that? The fact that his glasses had been removed and apparently tossed to one side?'

Williams frowned, dropping his head slightly.

'You suggesting I don't know how to do my job, Mr. Rednapp?'

'Not at all, Deputy Williams. It just seems to me that this glasses business doesn't tally with the story of a simple accident.'

He settled back, momentarily pacified.

'Hard to say what happened out there, sir, based on the evidence. Probably took them off and then accidentally dropped them. He wouldn't have been able to find them because he couldn't see properly. Maybe that was how he died, stumbling around feeling for them and not being aware how close he was to the edge.'

'The glasses had an elastic strap that held them onto his head while he was out riding his bike, isn't that so?'

'Yeah, they did. The strap was still on 'em.'

'And it's my understanding that he had to wear the glasses whenever he was out in bright sunlight.'

'That's what I understand, too. From his parents.'

I looked up.

'Then why would he have taken off his glasses in the first place?'

Deputy Williams shifted uncomfortably in his chair.

'How should I know? Maybe he took them off to clean them. Maybe he got sea spray on them.'

'Maybe,' I said. I checked my notes. 'That vista point. Any idea why Leo would have stopped there in the first place?'

'Nope. Other than tourists the only people that use that parking area are local young people looking for a place to make out or to smoke dope.'

'Do you think Leo Walensky would've stopped there for either of those reasons?'

The deputy grinned.

'No, sir. Not likely. Far as I know he had no girlfriend. And he certainly wasn't one to use narcotics.'

'Well, one thing's sure, Deputy. Leo Walensky couldn't see well enough to enjoy the view, could he? So he wouldn't have stopped for that.'

Williams looked uneasy.

'Probably not.'

I nodded.

'So we don't really know what he was doing at that vista point, do we?'

'No, sir.'

I made another note.

'You say some young person told you they'd seen Leo bicycling out from town in that direction, is that right?'

'Yep. Kid named Harlan Watts. His dad owns the general store across from the vista point road. Harlan's the same age as Leo, same year in school.'

'Did he say anything about the way the Walensky boy looked? Was there anything unusual about him? Was he carrying anything with him on the bike?'

'Nothing unusual, no. Harlan said he was wearing his rucksack, but then he always rode around with that on his back, to carry water and stuff.'

'Did you find the rucksack at the cliff edge?'

The deputy sat back, his mouth opening.

'Ah... No, I didn't. To be honest, I never thought about it. I guess I just assumed it went into the sea with him when he fell.'

'It would probably still have been on him when he was found if that was the case, wouldn't it?'

Williams looked irritated.

'Maybe. Maybe not. Maybe he'd taken it off to get a drink of water and carried it over with him when he fell. How should I know?

In any case, there was no rucksack out there.'

'What about his cell phone? Did you find that on his body when it was brought up?'

'Nope. There was no cell phone either.'

'My understanding was that he always carried one.'

The Deputy shrugged.

'Stands to reason. Most kids do.'

'So there was no cell phone, and no rucksack. If he was wearing the rucksack when he went over the edge the chances are he would've still been wearing it when he was found. Don't you think?'

'Don't know. Probably. How should I know?'

'But you say it wasn't there.'

He glared at me.

'That's right. There was no rucksack.'

'Look, Deputy Williams,' I said, trying to find a mollifying tone, 'I'm not trying to make it look like you didn't do your job right ...'

'That's what you're doing right enough,' he interrupted, tersely.

'Well, I'm sorry if I give that impression because I don't mean to.' I leaned toward him. 'But the fact is I wouldn't be here if everything looked as straightforward as you seem to think it is. There was no reason, as I understand it, for Leo Walensky to have committed suicide. And he was far too clever to have stepped out beyond that railing without his glasses. See what I mean? For another thing, you told my editor the boy wasn't particularly liked by quite a lot of people in this town. Can you tell me what that was all about?'

Deputy Williams sat back, scratched his elbow.

'Well, I think I probably made too much of that when I spoke to your boss. There was ... there's been ... some talk about how he was making a lot of people mad with the way he was spouting off his crazy atheistic ideas. Kid was bright, but also a bit arrogant. Thought he had a right to lecture people on their beliefs and try to undermine their faith.'

I raised my eyebrows.

'Leo was an atheist? Was that it?'

'That's right. And he wouldn't shut up about it. Kept telling people that belief in God was what was turning the world into the cesspit it is at the moment. One creed pitted against another, one religion against another. Like that. Kept saying the only way things would change was if people gave up religion and the idea of an afterlife altogether and started living as if this is the only existence we've got, accepting their own responsibility for deciding what's right and wrong, trying to make the best of what living has to offer without hurting anybody else or causing them any inconvenience.'

I nodded. 'Sounds a pretty sensible philosophy to me. Why did people react so violently against it?

Williams looked down at the floor, turning his hat in his hands.

'You don't know Shelter Cove, Mr. Rednapp. This ain't San Francisco. This is a Christian community. Very few people in this town who aren't firm church-going folk. I guess they just got tired of hearing the boy badmouth God.'

I raised my eyebrows again.

'And did what? Killed him to shut him up?'

Williams bristled.

'No, sir! Of course not! I mean they turned against him for what he was saying. Some of them did anyway. But that was all there was to it. People were looking forward to him leaving Shelter Cove, going off to college, so they wouldn't have to listen to his crazy ideas anymore.'

I nodded.

'He was bound for college in the fall, was he?'

'Yes. Got accepted by some big university down in the Bay area.'

I made another note, then looked up.

'You said that people were tired of listening to his ideas – the townspeople, I mean. What did you mean by that? How did they get to know his ideas? Did he preach on street corners? Hold meetings? What?'

Williams sniggered.

'Might as well have. Did the next best thing. Wrote a newsletter that he published himself every other week – a little broadsheet called '*The Humanist*' that he used to print out somehow and stuff into folks's mailboxes in the night so's no one would know who did it, who was responsible. Had his own private crusade, it seems, trying to turn the whole town into thinking like he did.'

I reached into my jacket and pulled out the folded sheet of crumpled paper.

'This one of them? I found it this afternoon.'

The deputy stood and took the page from me, opening it up and frowning down at it.

'Yep, that's one of them. The last one it looks like, from the date at the top.' He looked up at me. 'Where'd you find it?'

'It was balled up and caught in the branches of a bush by the side of the vista point parking lot.'

The deputy stared at me, then down at the page again.

'That blood, do you think?'

'Don't know, Deputy. Think you'd better check it out?'

Williams folded the paper and slid it into the shirt pocket next to his badge.

'I'll do that. You don't mind me taking it, do you?'

'Not at all. Better to know than not to know. And if it is blood, whose it is. Don't you think?'

'I do.' He turned for the door, settling his deputy's hat on his red thatch.

I stood up.

'What are the Walenskys like as a family, Deputy? Do you know them?'

He turned back. 'Leo's family?'

I nodded.

He shrugged. 'Decent enough people. Connie Walensky's the local dentist. His wife Muriel's the librarian. She only works part time, though.'

'Any other kids?'

'A daughter, about ten. Sweet kid, as I remember.'

'Anything else you can tell me about them as a family?'

He shook his head.

'Just normal folk. Lived here long as I can remember. Leo was born here – or in the hospital in Fortuna, rather. So was his sister. Nice people. They didn't deserve what happened.'

'Who does?'

He nodded, settled his shoulders, looked me in the eye.

'You going to be in town for a while?'

'For a couple days, at least.'

'Let me know when you intend to go.'

'I'll do that. And if you would, please let me know what you learn about the smudge on that paper.'

For a long time he just stood at the door, looking at me as if he couldn't quite make me out. Then he nodded.

'All right. I'll do that.'

I stood up and extended my hand. Williams shook it.

'I might want to see a few folks here in town, to ask a few questions,' I told him. 'Will that bother you, Deputy?'

'Not at all. Not unless you make a nuisance of yourself, get people's dander up. I'd have to run you off if you did that.' He smiled.

I nodded. 'I'll try not to.'

Then he opened the door and stepped out into the dusk.

I called Abe Rawlings and filled him in on what I'd learned so far. He chewed it over.

'You think my instinct was right?' he asked, finally.

'Don't know yet, Abe. But there are certainly some questions that need answering. I can keep myself busy here for a couple days yet. Who knows what I'll turn up.'

'Well,' he said, 'if there's anything there I know you'll find it.

Look after yourself, Arnold.'

And the line went dead.

At just after eight that evening I was seated in a booth at the Cove Restaurant finishing off a good sirloin steak, salad and fries when a couple of figures suddenly loomed over my table. I looked up. Two men: one short and tentative, wearing a baseball cap and a light jacket, the other taller, bigger, athletic, and very self-assured, wearing a blue plaid Pendleton shirt. It was the latter who spoke.

'Mr. Rednapp? My name's Dale Anders. This here's Gus Willis. Gus is the Mayor of Shelter Cove. I own this restaurant.'

I nodded. 'Gentlemen.' And smiled. 'What can I do for you, Coach?'

Anders' eyes narrowed, then he looked around. The place was relatively quiet. The dinner rush had thinned out an hour before and there were only a few tables and booths occupied around the room.

'Mind if we join you?' he asked at last, looking down at me again. 'There's something we'd like to talk to you about.'

I nodded to the empty space opposite.

'Be my guest.'

They slid onto the banquette, the mayor first, still wearing his baseball cap. When they'd settled, Anders hunched forward over the tabletop and crossed his arms, looking over at me.

'I hear you're in town asking about what happened out at the point. Is that right?'

'Yes, that's correct.'

'Why?'

I took a sip from my glass of Napa Valley red.

'I'm a reporter, Mr. Anders. I look for news. The death of that boy is news, sad as it may be.'

Anders scoffed. 'News for us, maybe. For the folks up in Eureka. But not for city folk a couple hundred miles away. They've got their own tragedies to read about.'

'So you know where I'm from?'

Anders sat back.

'The *South Bay Bulletin*, I believe.'

There was only one way Anders could have known that. From Deputy Williams. I was slightly disappointed by that, but not too surprised.

'Now what could a hotshot reporter from one of the state's most notorious scandal sheets find in a simple accidental death that could justify such attention so far from home?' Anders asked finally.

I pushed my plate to one side, wiped my hands on my napkin and dropped it on the plate, then leant forward towards him.

'What is it you want, Mr. Anders? Is there some reason you don't like me doing my job?'

He glared at me a moment.

'This is a nice community, Mr. Rednapp. Shelter Cove residents are nice people. They obey the law and they pay their taxes and they support all the right charities. We don't have much in the way of crime going on around here, and for a very good reason. Everyone here believes in two things: in working hard, and in minding their own business.'

I'd heard that before from Lorraine. It must be some kind of local litany.

'They're all God-fearing Christians, too, are they not?'

He sat back.

'Why, yes they are, Mr. Rednapp. So far as I know all the residents of this town are good Christian folk.'

'Except for Leo Walensky.'

Anders' mouth became a hard line.

'What's that supposed to mean?'

I sat back and took another sip of wine.

'I believe it's well known that the boy was an outspoken atheist. That must not have sat well with a lot of the local residents. Am I right?'

He glared at me again, longer this time.

'If you think because people took exception to his wild Godless ideas that they would actually do something to him for it, you're well off the mark, mister. Anyway, the boy was due to head off to college in a few days. There'd be no reason.'

'Suggesting that there *would* be a reason if he hadn't been going away?'

Anders leaned forward again, menacingly.

'I don't like your attitude, Rednapp.'

I smiled again.

'Can't say I'm wildly enamoured of yours, Anders. So what now? Are you going to threaten me with some dire punishment if I don't immediately drop my enquiry and skedaddle back to the Bay area? Is that the purpose of this interview?'

Anders sat back and the two men exchanged a quick, nervous glance.

'Of course not,' he said finally, his tone now more appeasing. 'You've got to understand, Mr. Rednapp, this community is just as shocked and saddened by what happened to that boy as anyone down in the city would be. But what happened out there on the point was just an accident, a simple accident. That's all. Leo Walensky was only partially sighted. Obviously he dropped his glasses and inadvertently walked over the cliff edge. It's sad, but that's all that happened.'

'Why was he out near the cliff edge in the first place, Mr. Anders? Have you asked yourself that?'

The big man ignored me.

'Gus and I are here because we're just concerned citizens, Mr. Rednapp. Shelter Cove's economy depends on tourism, on attracting people to come here to fish our streams and our surf and to walk our mountain paths and beaches. When they do that, they also use our stores and motels and restaurants. If you go down south and write some half-baked nonsense about 'suspicious circumstances' surrounding the boy's death it could do us all a lot of harm. The town's reputation would be tarnished and for no good reason. Because *there's nothing here for you to find,* Mr. Rednapp!' Anders emphasized the point by tapping the table firmly with his forefinger on every word. 'That boy died purely through misadventure,' he went on. 'There was no one else involved but him, and if you carry on this investigation you're just wasting your own time and bringing a lot of unnecessary pain and worry to us.' He sat back, crossed his arms, settling himself. 'That's why we're here, sir. To ask you to desist from bringing our town's reputation down unjustly.'

I nodded. Picking up my wineglass I drained it, then replaced it with precision on the tabletop in front of me.

'I'll make you a deal, Anders. I'm a fair man and the last thing I want to do is cause any problems for your town without justification.' I looked him in the eye. 'I promise you that I will publish nothing about Shelter Cove unless and until I find clear and unassailable proof of something unsavory relating to that boy's death. If it was simply an accident, or a suicide, then regardless of the bad feeling some folk here held toward him I'll go away and forget the whole thing. Bad feeling in itself is not news. Murder is.'

After a moment Anders smiled, looked at Willis, who nodded his head almost imperceptibly. Then Anders looked back at me.

'There's been no murder, Mr. Rednapp. I'm sure of that. But I'll ask one more thing of you, if you'll be so kind. I'd like you to come to me first with anything you find that does seem ... suspicious or untoward in this matter. I mean, before you talk to anyone else. I might be able to explain it, you see? Will you do that?'

I considered, then nodded my head.

'I'll do that.'

He reached inside his jacket and produced a card, which he handed to me.

'This's my card as owner of the restaurant. My cell number's on it. You can call me anytime.'

Then the two men slid out of the booth and left.

30

3.

The motel bed was comfortable and I slept late the next morning, tired from the long drive and the events of the previous day. When I awoke the sky was still clear outside and shafts of bright sunlight angled through the gaps in my window curtains. Trying to hold to my usual routine, I took a half hour seaside jog along the sandy stretch that extended to the south of the town beyond the cove. Smell of salt water, screeching seagulls, light glinting off the surf as it crashed in frothy waves onto the narrow beach. A couple of people out exercising their dogs greeted me as I passed them. I got the feeling I was recognized.

I've always enjoyed being at the edge of the sea. I guess that comes from growing up inland, hundreds of miles away from it – the thought of all that water and the wonderful exotic places far away on the other side of it still gives me the shivers.

Back at the motel I showered and dressed and at eleven o'clock walked the two hundred yards from the motel to the Cove, where I found my usual booth overlooking the sea and sat down to peruse the menu. I was still deciding when Lorraine appeared at my elbow, carrying the coffeepot.

'Hey,' I said. 'Morning, gorgeous.'

'Good morning yourself.' She smiled. 'Coffee?'

'You bet. Hot and black.'

'Like your women?'

'Ha! You've got an overactive imagination.'

She filled the cup she held in her free hand and set it before me.

'Oh, I know about you Bay area types. You're into all sorts.' She stepped back, putting down the coffeepot and raising her order book. 'So, what're you having this morning?'

I took another quick look at the menu.

'A short-stack of buttermilks with an egg over easy and some bacon on the side. Oh, and a glass of O.J. I need to keep healthy.'

She looked at me over her notepad.

'You look healthy enough to me.'

'Thanks. I missed you last night. Another nice lady served me instead.'

'That would have been Ardelle. She's on nights this week. She's a sweetheart.' She finished writing the order and picked up the coffeepot. 'She's married, though, hon. You're better off with me.'

'I'll remember that,' I told her, grinning.

'You'd better,' she said, moving off.

She had travelled almost halfway back to the counter when she suddenly stopped and retraced her steps.

'I forgot,' she said.

'Forgot what?'

'I asked my daughter last night if she knew anything about the Walensky boy. She said he was responsible for the handbills that have been pushed into our mailbox every couple of weeks for the last month or two.'

'That's right. Did you read the handbills?'

'Not really. I skimmed them and threw them out. Thought it was probably some local crackpot trying to stir up trouble. Mandy told me it was widely believed that Leo Walensky had written and delivered them, and that a lot of people in the community were angry about it.'

'So it seems. Thanks for telling me, Lorraine.'

'No problem. Hope it's useful.'

She turned with a smile and went off with the coffee pot.

While I was waiting for my order I pulled out my notepad and looked over my notes. The night before I had started making a list of the people I felt I had to see today. At the top of the list was the Walensky family, followed by two other entries: 'Friends?' and 'Enemies?' I had run out of known contacts to chase – except for Leo's family. It was time to make myself known to them and get their side of the story. Today was Sunday. I reckoned that if I left it till after lunch I'd probably find them home from church – if they went to church. After that I decided I'd pretty much play it by ear as to who to see next – hopefully with guidance from them.

The breakfast, when it came, was as good as the rest of the meals I'd had at the Cove. I ate it leisurely, then sat back as Lorraine cleared away the plates and refreshed my coffee.

'You going to be busy later, Arnie? Or are you taking a break from work on the Lord's day?'

'There's no rest for the wicked,' I told her. 'No, I'll be out there digging around. For a while, anyway.' I sipped my coffee while she wiped the table. 'You religious, Lorraine?'

'Me?' she scoffed. 'Not hardly. I was raised a Methodist, but gave it up long ago.' She made a face. 'Couldn't stand the smug company. Or the hypocrisy.'

'I know the feeling. Can I ask you another question?'

'If it's about whether I'm free tonight, the answer's yes. My ex came last night and took my daughter away for a few days.'

'Well, that *is* interesting, but it's not what I wanted to know.'

'Oh. Pity.'

'What I'm wondering is if you can tell me where I can find the Walensky home, where the boy Leo lived with his parents? I've got their address, but I'm still finding my way around here and I'd appreciate your help.'

She stood by the table, holding the coffeepot and staring down at me.

'Boy, you're in for a fun day, I can tell. I should hang in there. You might well need company by tonight.'

'I might indeed. In the meantime, can you help me?'

She sighed.

'I'll draw you a map. Their place is just at the edge of town. One of the older, original houses. Can't miss it.'

She went off, and came back five minutes later with a pencil sketch map of the bay and the main town streets, with an 'x' marking the spot where I'd find the Walensky house, standing on its own apart from the others. At the bottom of the map was Lorraine's name and a cell phone number.

I folded up the map and put it in my pocket.

I had some time to kill so I left the car at the motel and took a walk along the frontage road to the north. Cliff and sea on one side, nice modern ranch-style houses with wide, well-kept lawns on the other. A block or two along I came to a cyclone fence that enclosed a playground and the long, single-story pale yellow building that was the Shelter Cove Elementary School. As I came abreast of the driveway I could see a lone car parked outside the main entrance with its trunk lid open. A tall, middle-aged lady in a colorful print summer dress was just coming through the school door carrying a cardboard box. On a whim, I turned into the entrance and walked up to her as she slid the box into the car's trunk.

'Morning,' I opened, 'anything I can help you with, Ma'am?'

She stood back and looked me over, brushing wayward strands of greying hair back from her forehead with one hand. I guess she approved of me because she didn't scream or run away.

'You can help me carry another couple of boxes out here to the car, if you have the time,' she said evenly.

'Sure thing.'

I followed her inside the building and into a glassed-in office space at the end of a long corridor with classroom doors opening off on either side. A counter separated the reception part of the office from the secretary's desk and the principal's office door beyond. She led me around the counter and through the open door into the principal's room, which was clearly hers. Two more boxes were on her desk, stuffed full of files and box files. She took the smaller and I the larger and we retraced our steps out to the car. When we had placed them beside the others in the trunk, she closed the lid and rubbed her hands together.

'Thank you for that. They're pupil files. I have to make sure all the records have been properly brought up to date before the new school year starts in a few days' time. It's easier to do that at home.'

'I thought it was probably something like that.'

She looked at me again, more closely this time.

'You're not from around here. A tourist? Or visiting someone locally?'

'Neither, as it happens.' I pulled out one of my cards and gave it to her. 'Arnold Rednapp. I'm a reporter from a small South San Francisco paper. I'm here to look into the death of the Walensky boy.'

She glanced up from the card and her face clouded with genuine sadness.

'Leo. Yes. Such a lovely young man.' She returned the card and I slipped it back into my wallet. 'Hazel Mendoza,' she said, extending her hand, which I shook. 'I'm the Principal of the school.'

'So I gathered,' I said, smiling.

'Any particular reason why a Bay area reporter should be covering an accidental death in a tiny town hundreds of miles away?'

I used the same line I'd given Lorraine.

'Human interest. Apart from that there're some circumstances surrounding the boy's death that need to be looked into. It could have been an accident. But there's an outside chance that it could also have been something else.'

Hazel Mendoza frowned.

'Murder?'

'Too early to say. That's why I'm here. To find out.'

She nodded. Then she looked around and turned to glance back toward the school.

'I have to lock up. Want a quick cup of coffee? I can make you some instant, if that won't turn your stomach.'

'Coffee would be fine, Mrs. Mendoza.' I had noticed the wedding ring on her finger. 'And one cup of instant won't kill me.'

Ten minutes later we were seated in her office with mugs in our hands – she behind her desk, me opposite her in the chair usually filled by errant children. For instant the coffee was good.

'So,' she said at length, 'tell me about these strange things relating to Leo's death.'

I outlined briefly the anomalies I had encountered thus far: the jettisoned glasses, the lost cell phone and rucksack, the lack of any clear explanation as to why Leo would have stopped at the vista point in the first place, or in any case why he would've stepped out onto the cliff edge.

'There's one other thing,' I concluded. 'As you probably know, Leo hadn't made himself popular with the townspeople over the summer with his atheistic broadsheets. Some of the locals, I gather, got quite hot under the collar about it.'

Mrs. Mendoza smiled tightly.

'Yes, that's true. But I hardly think they're angry enough to resort to murder.'

'Hopefully not, but the possibility still remains – at least until I find answers to the questions raised.'

She nodded, sipped her coffee. So did I.

'In the meantime,' I continued, 'since I've discovered you by chance, could you tell me a bit about the boy, Mrs. Mendoza? You must have known him for years – that is, if you've been here that long.'

'Oh, yes. I've been here that long. Twenty years this month. Yes, I watched Leo grow up.' She rested her cup on the desk and sat back, crossing her arms. 'Where to start? Leo was always a pleasant boy, and very bright – an exceptional pupil – but his limited vision made it difficult for him to join in with the rest of the boys in outdoor games, so he became a loner. He also tended to be introverted. He apparently liked his own company and actually made few close friends among his peers. Of course, the children knew about Leo's eyes, and for the most part they were sympathetic. Sometimes, though, there were the inevitable taunts and insults – especially when he proved to be so much better in his studies than the others. But Leo ignored them, and finally the taunts stopped. In spite of his affliction, he was basically a well-adjusted, very happy boy.'

'What about the girls? Did he make friends with any of them?'

'More with them than with the boys, but nothing very close or long-lasting. At least, not so far as I know. You have to remember I was his principal, not one of his teachers. They would be in a better position than me to know about that.'

By this time I had produced my notebook and was scribbling notes.

'What about his atheistic beliefs? Any idea where they came from?'

She shook her head.

'No. And it's a little strange, since neither his mother nor his father are atheists – to my knowledge.' She took another sip from her coffee cup and leaned forward over the desk. 'There is something I could tell you though that might be useful. It has always been my feeling that Leo Walensky suffered from a slight degree of autism, or something like it – I'm not very knowledgeable about these things, I admit. Not enough to be diagnosed as such, to be sure, but enough to make him slightly ... unusual in his behavior. To make him a bit irritable and frustrated at times – about the difficulties he faced because of his eyes – and to occasionally make him obsessive about things. Leo was never one to do anything by halves. If he took an interest in something he had to spend all his time on it, until he had exhausted its potential and he could move on to something new. I've always felt, in a way, that his atheism was a bit like that – a reasonable enough point of view philosophically, but much more extreme in his case than was necessary. It's one thing to embrace a philosophy or belief wholeheartedly, but quite another to decide to turn your life into a crusade to change the minds of everyone around you into adopting your position. I wasn't too bothered by his broadsheets because I always reckoned that when Leo got to university this drive to convert everyone around him would stop and he would regain his equilibrium.'

'Well, he didn't get his chance to do that, unfortunately,' I said.

'No,' she said. 'Sadly he didn't.'

I finished writing and closed the notebook. 'Thanks, Mrs. Mendoza.' I stood up and placed the empty coffee cup on her desk. 'You've been very helpful. Thanks, too, for the coffee.'

She smiled and stood with me.

'Thank you for the help with the boxes. If there's anything else I can do for you just let me know. My number's in the book. My husband's the local plumber.'

'I'll bear that in mind,' I said.

We walked together to the school entrance door, where we shook hands once again.

'It's been nice talking with you, Mr. Rednapp. Good luck with your investigation.'

'I hope you have a great school year, Mrs. Mendoza,' I said with a smile, and turned to make my way back to the motel.

I wasn't looking forward to my interview with Leo's family, but it had to be done. I had to know more about the boy, who his friends were now, *if* he had friends. I wanted to know if he had picked up his beliefs from his parents, or if they'd come from some other source. If so, I thought it was important to find out who or what that source was. It wasn't going to be easy, but it wasn't the first time I'd be dealing with recently bereaved parents, either. I'd just have to be tactful.

At two o'clock I slipped on my jacket, smoothed my hair and left the motel to take the car the few blocks to the Walenskys' house.

The breeze off the ocean kept the ambient temperature in the mid-seventies, which was perfect. Terrible to think of people having to suffer grief in such wonderful weather – it's almost a kind of slap in the face.

On one of the central thoroughfares a white church with a traditional pointed steeple stood in the middle of a broad lawn. The church doors were open, and a white cassocked reverend and a cluster of people stood on the steps nearby in their Sunday best jawing. Someone among them called attention to my car and suddenly all the faces turned in my direction. The faces were not wearing friendly smiles. I waved and smiled back at them, however, and drove on by.

The Walensky house was an old two-story clapboard affair with a roofed front porch and a flight of wooden steps leading up to it. I parked in the street before the narrow front lawn and walked up the cement pavement toward it. At the left side of the lawn was a driveway leading to a garage at the side of the house. A tan Volvo station wagon was parked in front of it. There was a smaller economy car parked on the street in front of mine. I wondered if that was for Mrs. Walensky's use. As I climbed the stairs I could hear not a sound from the house. With some trepidation I crossed to the screened front door and pressed the doorbell. It was a long couple of minutes before the door finally opened and a haggard looking man of about fifty in a white shirt and wrinkled chinos stood staring out at me. Like his son, Connie Walensky wore glasses. He had also lost most of his hair.

'Yes?'

'Mr. Walensky? I'm awfully sorry to bother you, sir, but I wonder if you could spare me a few minutes?'

I took out my card and pushed it through the gap at the side of the screen door. He took it and lifted it up to read.

'I'm a reporter, Mr. Walensky. From the *South Bay Bulletin*, in the Bay area. Your wife's brother, Abe Rawlings, is my editor, my boss. He's sent me up here to cover the death of your son, Leo – for which, of course, I offer my most sincere condolences.'

'Thank you,' he said, pushing the card back out through the gap. 'Your boss is a good man. Highly regarded as a journalist. So's your paper. It does good work.'

'I'm glad you think so.'

'Abe didn't tell us you were coming. Why is it he's sent you all the way up here to cover just an accident, Mr. Rednapp?' Mr. Walensky cocked his head to one side. 'Or does Abe think it wasn't just an accident?'

'Well, sir. There are some curious circumstances related to the death, as I'm sure you're aware. This is just a routine investigation. There's probably nothing, but I've been asked to look into it.'

Mr. Walensky nodded. Then he pushed open the screen and stepped aside.

'Come on in, Mr. Rednapp. It's a pretty somber house just now, as I'm sure you can appreciate, but I guess we can give you a few minutes.'

'Thank you, sir.'

Mr. Walensky led me into the large front room and pointed to a couch.

'Have a seat, Mr. Rednapp. I'll get Muriel. She's ... resting.'

I nodded and sat on the sofa. While I waited I looked around me, getting a feel of the place. The room's decor was in keeping with the age of the house itself – a few tasteful antiques here and there (Tiffany lamps and upholstered armchairs with antimacassars, some Persian carpets and what looked to be a walnut chiffonier against one wall), and some other more modern furniture pieces bought obviously for comfort and convenience – including a pair of tall pine bookcases filled with a wide range of books. It was obviously a house where people read a lot. It was also a cozy house, and felt very homey on first view. As I sat there I could hear the murmur of a young girl's voice somewhere above me, seemingly playing at something. Apart from that a heavy atmosphere of grief and pain resonated through the silent rooms.

It was fully five minutes before Mr. Walensky reappeared, supporting on his arm a woman wearing a pale yellow dressing gown, her face still red from weeping. She'd obviously made an effort to pull herself together, though – splashed cold water on her face and tidied her hair – and now she pulled herself free from her husband's arm and stood erect, forcing a half-smile of greeting.

'Good afternoon, Mr. Rednapp.'

I stood.

'Mrs. Walensky. I'm so sorry for your loss.'

She waved away my words.

'Thank you, sir. Please be seated. Would you like some coffee?'

'No, thank you, Ma'am. I'm fine.'

I sat again, as did they, in two matching armchairs that must have been their regular places in the room. Mr. Walensky stretched out one hand, into which Mrs. Walensky placed hers. They sat looking at me like that with their hands clasped.

'Our daughter Amy is upstairs playing, Mr. Rednapp,' the exhausted woman said. 'Ordinarily I'd invite her down to say 'hello', but under the circumstances I think it's best to leave her alone. She's taking all this ... very badly.'

I nodded. 'I totally agree. Let her play.'

'So what can we do for you, sir? Connie tells me you're from down south, from Abe's paper?'

'That's right, Mrs. Walensky. He sent me up here to do a piece about your son, and I was hoping you might be able to answer a few questions for me.'

'Well,' she looked at her husband, 'I think we can do that. Or at least try. What do you want to know?'

I pulled out my notepad and pen and got myself ready.

'Firstly, just to confirm, Leo was seventeen years old, and had just graduated from Fortuna High School, is that correct?'

'That's right,' his father returned. 'With honors. We were going to take him down to start his first year at Stanford in a few days' time.'

'Stanford, eh? Then he really was a good student.'

'An excellent student,' his mother said. 'He had the choice of several different top class universities.'

'During his high school years did he have any teachers he was particularly fond of, or subjects that were of special interest to him?'

'Well,' Mr. Walensky began, 'all his teachers liked him, we know that. But as far as there being anyone particularly valued by my son ... perhaps his biology teacher last year, Miss Evans? Oh, and his Senior English teacher, Guy Abbott.'

I made my notes.

'Any particular reason for his special fondness for these people? Was it something in what they taught, or how they taught?'

'I'm not sure I can answer that,' Mr. Walensky returned. 'I know he found biology fascinating. He talked about it often, loved working in the lab with microscopes studying one-celled life. I think that was part of it, certainly, where Miss Evans was concerned. As for Mr. Abbott, apart from Leo telling me he found the man very inspiring in his teaching methods, he's also a gifted chess player. Leo had two passions, Mr. Rednapp: reading and chess. Guy Abbott offered both these attractions. He managed to make Leo want to read every book he ever mentioned, both in class and outside. And more often than not Leo did read them. He was a voracious reader, my son.'

Beside him his wife stifled a sob and he gripped her hand even more tightly.

'Sorry, Mrs. Walensky,' I said, gently. 'I'll try not to keep you much longer.'

'I'm fine,' she said, dropping her husband's hand and sitting up. 'Please, carry on.'

'So Leo liked playing chess?' I asked, after a moment.

'That's right,' his father said. 'He got too good for me over the last couple of years. I couldn't give him a game anymore. That's why he got so friendly with Guy Abbott. Guy was a minor champion in his youth and had a lot to teach Leo. They often played during lunch hours, and sometimes Leo would stay after school a couple hours and take the late afternoon bus home. You should talk to him.'

'I will. There's a bus service to Shelter Cove from Fortuna then?'

'Twice a day. Eight in the morning and six at night.'

'I see.' I made some notes, then looked up. 'Your son was an atheist, is that right?'

The two of them exchanged a guarded glance.

'Yes, he was,' Mr. Walensky confirmed. 'He's been ... was ... an atheist ever since he was a small boy.'

I looked up from my notepad.

'His conversion to atheism had nothing to do with Mr. Abbott?'

'Oh, no,' Mr. Walensky replied. 'Guy's progressive opinions might have reinforced Leo's anti-religious sentiments, but he wasn't the one who initiated them.'

'Okay. Was it Mr. Abbott that introduced Leo to the philosophy of the Humanists?'

Walensky looked at his wife, then back at me.

'I believe so,' he said at last. 'At least, he gave Leo several Humanist authors to read, some pretty heavy stuff. They're upstairs in his room now, the books. It was after that that Leo suddenly announced to us that he was a Humanist.'

'Not so strange a choice for an atheist. Are the two of you non-believers as well?'

Connie Walensky shook his head.

'No. Muriel attends the Quaker Meeting House in Fortuna regularly. As for me, I was raised a Catholic.' He half smiled. 'The son of Polish immigrants, you see? Although, like many Catholics these days I hardly ever attend Mass.'

'You didn't raise Leo as a Catholic, then?'

Walensky sighed. 'I signed an undertaking to, with the church. But Leo wouldn't have it, even as a boy of six. Even then he rejected the idea of believing in anything he couldn't see for himself, anything that couldn't be proven to exist.'

'That must have been awkward for you?'

Leo's father shrugged.

'What could I do? He was a boy with a very strong will. Once he'd decided something he'd stick to it come hell or high water.'

I made some more notes, then glanced up at them again.

'I've been told that there was some bad feeling in the town toward your son because of his beliefs and opinions. Is that so?'

'Yes,' Walensky replied after a moment. 'People thought it wrong for so young a man to harbor such ... un-Christian ideas.'

'How did they find out about Leo's beliefs? Was he so open about them?'

Walensky looked to his wife, who sighed and then took up the story.

'You have to understand, Mr. Rednapp,' she said, producing a handkerchief from the sleeve of her dressing gown. 'My son was an exceptional young man. He had a very high I.Q. and would've gone far in this world if he'd had the chance.' She lifted the handkerchief and dabbed at her eyes. 'He was also very sensitive, both as a boy and as a young man. He observed the terrible events on the evening news and drew his own conclusions about their causes. As he grew older and read ... certain books ... he began to feel he had a mission in life. If there is ever going to be a change in the way people live, he thought, a change that can prevent the senseless suffering and hatred, death and destruction in this world, then people will have to accept a new way of seeing themselves and their lives, a way that excludes belief in any divinity and puts the onus of determining what is right and wrong squarely upon the shoulders of each individual, without the guidance of any dogma or dictate – relying simply upon common sense and conscience. Leo believed in that wholeheartedly. He'd also come to believe that it was his job – in a small way – to do what he could to spread the word.'

'That 'word' being the potential danger of all religious belief, and the true value of an empirically based practical philosophy of life, such as that embraced by the Humanists?'

'Exactly.'

'I see. And how did he intend to reach his ... his audience ... to bring about this conversion?'

Both parents sat up in their chairs.

'Mr. Rednapp,' Mrs. Walensky said, 'my son had no gifts as an orator, nor did he have the self-confidence to be one. What he did have was his brain, and his ability to write clearly and persuasively. Apparently he decided six months or so ago to put his ideas down on paper and to ... to spread them around in the community surreptitiously – to give people food for thought, rock the boat a little. We knew nothing of this at the time – he didn't mention it to us. Only later did we find out who was responsible for the strange broadsheets that suddenly began appearing every other week in our mailbox.'

Mrs. Walensky turned to the low chest of drawers beside her, opened the middle of three drawers and produced a sheaf of papers gathered together in a clear plastic sleeve. Rising, she stepped across the room to hand the papers to me.

'These are the broadsheets he printed, Mr. Rednapp. I've saved them all – initially because I was intrigued as to where they came from, later because I was proud of my son's ability to write so clearly and well.'

I took the pages out of the sleeve and glanced through them. They looked much like the one I had found at the vista point – same layout with '*The Humanist*' at the top over the date, same general format with recent news items of religious-inspired atrocities listed at the end. Carefully, I slipped them back into the sleeve.

'Would you mind if I kept these for a day or so, Mrs. Walensky? I'd really like to read them.'

'Not at all. Just take care of them, please. They've become ... quite important to me now.'

'Of course.' I laid the plastic sleeve to one side and picked up my notepad again. 'And you had no idea when they first started arriving that Leo had anything to do with them?'

They both shook their heads.

'People told us it was his work, but for a long time we couldn't believe it,' Mrs. Walensky said. 'He had no facilities here at home to mass produce such a document – there must have been hundreds of copies. But finally Connie and I realized that Leo had to be the source. We asked him about them then, and he confessed to us that he had written and printed them.'

'Apparently quite a few of the townspeople knew who was responsible,' Mr. Walensky added. 'Leo had spoken out often enough in school, and his classmates all knew of his anti-religious feelings and his Humanist sympathies. I'm sure they passed on their suspicions to their parents, and the tide of resentment and hatred against him – and us – started to build.'

I leaned forward.

'Did the local people come to you about it, try to persuade you to stop him doing what he was doing?'

'One or two of them did,' Mr. Walensky said, with a wry smile. 'Reverend Baker of the Episcopalian Church came around, ranting against the "heathen behavior" of our son, saying if we didn't make him stop immediately, and punish him soundly for his blasphemous carryings on, that we were all bound to suffer eternal perdition. I promised him that I would speak to Leo about it and he finally went away.'

'You also had a phone call from Coach Anders, Connie,' Mrs. Walensky reminded him.

Walensky nodded.

'Yes, I did. He was more to the point, left out the bit about eternal perdition. Just warned me that if Leo carried on with his broadsheets I might find I didn't have any local patients dropping into my dentistry anymore. Again, I told him I'd speak to Leo about it.'

'And did you?'

'Yes. Leo was saddened that there'd been such a negative reaction to his broadsheets from the community, and he tried to persuade me to ignore the threats. In any case, he said, he would soon be going away and the broadsheets would stop. Then life could get more or less back to normal around here.' Walensky looked up at me, slowly rubbing one hand with the other in his lap. 'That was two weeks ago. Last week was supposed to be the last page he was putting out. But so far as I can see, he never managed to get it printed and distributed.'

Something clicked in my head.

'Last week? You say the last newsletter was never delivered?'

'Apparently not. We didn't get one, which we usually did. Neither did our neighbors. Believe me, I would've heard about it if they had.'

I made some notes, frowning now with a mind crowded with possibilities.

'Do you have any idea where he got the broadsheets printed, or how they were distributed?'

The Walenskys exchanged a glance.

'No, we don't,' said the wife, shaking her head. 'He couldn't have printed them here because we only have an old inkjet printer. It is possible, though, that Leo did at least some of the delivering himself. This is a solid old house, and it's not impossible to creep out of it without being detected. But I honestly never heard him coming or going in the night.'

'Did he often go out riding his bike around the local area?'

'Yes. And sometimes he would use it to visit Leland.'

'Leland?'

'Leo has a friend a half-mile out past the vista point that he often visits,' Mr. Walensky contributed, immediately correcting himself. 'Visi-ted.'

I sat up straight.

'A friend? Can you tell me who that is? Someone from school?'

'Not from the high school, no,' Mr. Walensky went on. 'From the Shelter Cove Elementary School, where Leo went as a boy. The custodian of the school is a partly crippled Klamath Indian named Leland Whipple. Lee befriended Leo when he was eight or nine years old, offered to teach him how to fish. They often fished together off the rocks or in the surf, and sometimes Lee even took him north to the reservation – with our permission, of course – to fish with his tribes-people in their home waters on the Klamath. Leo loved it. Loved Leland. You should go see him. He can tell you a lot about our son. As can Guy Abbott.'

'I'll do that. I'll see them both.' I jotted Leland Whipple's name on the page, then looked up again. 'Was Leo on his way out to visit Whipple when he died, do you think?'

Mr. Walensky leaned forward.

'On his way back. He'd been out at the Whipples late that afternoon. Lee told us that when he called to ... to tell us how shocked and saddened he was to hear the news.'

I nodded.

'Did Leo have any other friends? Friends his own age?'

Walensky shook his head.

'Not so far as we know. No one close. Not since he was ten or twelve years old. There was a girl he liked back then, though. What was her name, Muriel?'

'Valerie. Valerie Rush. Lovely girl. Don't know why they didn't stay friends, but they just seemed to drift apart. She's still here in town. She's the girlfriend of Coach Anders' son, Bart. But as far as I know, they haven't had any close contact, she and Leo, for years.'

Connie Walensky's face had darkened at the mention of the coach's son. I wondered why.

'You frowned when Bart Anders was mentioned, Mr. Walensky. Any special reason for that, or is he just a not very nice young man? I should say I've met his father.'

Walensky let out his breath in a long slow blow.

'Dale Anders is an arrogant windbag, and his son is just like him. Both of them are opinionated bullies, and both of them made Leo's life hell at various times over the years.' He shook his head, darkly. 'No, I don't like him. Bart was the quarterback for the Fortuna football team, though, and very popular with the locals. Damn fools!'

'I see.' I made a note, then looked up again at the two grieving parents, putting as much sympathy in my face as I could muster.

'Mr. and Mrs. Walensky, do you think it's at all possible that your son took his own life?'

Their response was immediate.

'No!' Mr. Walensky said, firmly.

'Certainly not,' Mrs. Walensky added simultaneously, shaking her head. 'I told Abe when I called him that Leo had been in particularly good spirits over the last couple of weeks. I know he was excited about going to Stanford. His private life seemed somehow to have brightened up, too, for some reason, but he wouldn't tell me why. I was just glad to see him so happy and left it at that. No, Mr. Rednapp, I can categorically say that my son did not kill himself. There was no reason to.'

'What do you think about the accident idea? Could he have stepped too close to the edge and just fallen over?'

'Leo knew how dangerous those cliffs are, even to fully sighted people,' Mr. Walensky said. 'I can't imagine why he would have taken off his glasses in the first place. And then to have stepped beyond that barrier without them... Without the glasses he would hardly have been able to see.'

'So you think there was some other reason for his fall?'

The Walenskys looked again at one another and for a long moment neither spoke. Finally Mrs. Walensky broke the silence.

'Mr. Rednapp, we don't know what happened out there. All we know is that we no longer have Leo in our lives, and I cannot begin to tell you what a dreadful thing that is for all of us. If there was some other reason for him to have fallen from that cliff, we don't know what it could've been. It's hard to imagine that the irritation he caused the locals could have brought someone to actually do him harm. I simply can't believe that.' She sighed. 'So you see, we just don't know.'

I nodded, closed my notebook and stood up.

'Well, that's it – apart from...' I looked at them hesitantly. 'Would you mind if I had a quick glance at Leo's room? I'm trying to get a feel for the boy.'

'Sure,' Mr. Walensky returned. 'Why not?' He turned to his wife. 'You stay down here, honey. I'll make you a cup of tea in a minute. Okay?'

She nodded, smiling weakly at me.

'Help yourself, Mr. Rednapp,' she said. 'Leo's room is spotless. Always was. He was a very tidy boy. Very organized. You should have no trouble getting an idea of the kind of young man he was. And do drop by again before you leave Shelter Cove.'

'Thanks. I'll do that.' I lifted the plastic sleeve of papers. 'I'll have to return these in any case. I promise I'll look after them.'

She smiled and slumped gently back into the stuffed chair, watching us go.

Connie Walensky took me upstairs and left me in Leo's room while he stepped on down the hall. Mrs. Walensky was right. The room was very neat, and almost Spartan in its furnishings and decor. A giant poster of Beethoven was affixed to one wall, above his desk. Beside the desk the shelves of a low bookcase sagged with the weight of books. Apart from school texts and the usual assortment of popular novels and classics there were several hardback tomes, seemingly well-used, gathered together on the upper shelf. I glanced at the authors: Tom Paine and Thomas Jefferson, Ben Franklin, John Stuart Mill, Jean-Jacques Rousseau, Ernest Renan, Voltaire and Montesquieu, among others. I pulled out the *Age of Reason* of Tom Paine and leafed through the first few pages. Just inside the cover was a signature in a pinched handwriting: Guy Abbott. So. This was either his book on loan to the boy, or Abbott had given it to him as a present.

It was becoming clear where Leo had got his ideas.

On the lower shelf another collection of titles and authors caught my eye: books by Richard Dawkins and Christopher Hitchens, A.C. Grayling's *The God Argument* and *Das Kapital* by Karl Marx. I smiled at these last titles – thinking how the locals would have reacted had they known Leo was reading such things.

On the desk was a chess set with distinctive acrylic pieces representing medieval knights, kings and queens, bishops, castles and yeoman pawns spread across the board in mid-game positions. Beside it was a laptop, opened but dark. I wondered what I would find amongst its saved files if I flicked it on? But that would be invading Leo's privacy and I wasn't about to do that. Not if I could help it.

Mr. Walensky was waiting in the door when I turned around. He'd been in his tiny office along the hall, writing down the teacher Guy Abbott's contact details and drawing me a map of how to get to Leland Whipple's place. He gave me the page, which I glanced at, then folded and put in my pocket. Then he saw me down to the front door and out onto the porch.

'Stop by anytime, Mr. Rednapp,' he said. 'If there's anything more we can do for you.'

'Thanks for that, Mr. Walensky.'

'Please. Call me Connie.'

'And thanks for your help, Connie. Both you and your wife. It's much appreciated.'

I shook his hand and told him I was sorry I hadn't been able to know his son, as he seemed a remarkable young man who'd been destined for great things. Walensky said he was sure that was so and we said our goodbyes.

I headed back to the motel to go over all I had learned – from them, and from Mrs. Mendoza.

There was a lot to take in, a lot to fit together.

But, vaguely, a picture was beginning to take shape in my mind.

And it wasn't a pretty one.

4.

I spent an hour in my motel room skimming through Leo Walensky's writings, which were compelling reading – well reasoned arguments that tried, probably without much success, to introduce the local die-hard believers to a different way of thinking. There was nothing at all disrespectful or blasphemous in the writing, just an attempt to show it was time to at least consider something else. He probably hadn't made any converts but I admired him for having had a go.

I also liked his use of pertinent quotes, mostly from the nation's founding fathers (a swipe at the local Tea Party supporters?), pointing out the dangers of combining the business of government with any form of religion – even Christianity. The following are a few that I found particularly telling:

Thomas Jefferson: *"I have examined all the known superstitions of the world, and I do not find in our particular superstition of Christianity one redeeming feature. They are all alike founded on fables and mythology. Millions of innocent men, women and children, since the introduction of Christianity, have been burnt, tortured, fined and imprisoned. What has been the effect of this coercion? To make one half of the world fools and the other half hypocrites, to support roguery and error all over the earth."*

And James Madison: *"What influence in fact have Christian ecclesiastical establishments had on civil society? In many instances, they have been upholding the thrones of political tyranny. In no instance have they been seen as the guardians of the liberties of the people. Rulers who wished to subvert the public liberty have found in the clergy convenient auxiliaries. A just government, instituted to secure and perpetuate liberty, does not need the clergy."*

And finally, John Adams: *"The government of the United States is not in any sense founded on the Christian religion."*

August sentiments all, bound to give any intelligent man food for thought – if, that is, his mind is open to new and broadly unpopular ideas.

At four o'clock I put my notebook in my pocket, grabbed my jacket and headed for the car again. It was time to drive out to see Leland Whipple.

It had cooled slightly but was still perfect weather, and there were lots of tourists around the town who had driven out or flown to Shelter Cove for the day from up and down the coast. You could tell they were tourists from the fact that they were walking everywhere – exploring the cove, sauntering along the sea road past the school taking in the sights, or just standing in groups outside the busy cafés, restaurants and gift shops. The place was buzzing.

I ignored them all and drove back to the edge of town to take the turning opposite the general store.

It took ten minutes to get to the Whipple place. A hundred yards beyond the vista point turnout the road dropped down to flank a broad beach for half a mile, then climbed a low promontory that rose out of the sea, creating yet another cliff. The asphalt twisted its way on up through the trees, but I didn't take the road any further. Opposite the beach at that corner the Whipples' rough graveled drive led off to the right up a slope. Turning onto it I wound upwards for a few seconds until I came to a levelled parking area with a double-wide trailer home perched above it on the hillside. There was a battered red Toyota pickup parked in an open-sided garage below it. Beside the garage a flight of wooden steps led up to a deck that projected out from the trailer's front door to form a terrace overlooking the sea and the long stretch of beach. At the apex of the trailer's front gable, overlooking the parking area, a massive rack of elk horns was mounted on a board. Somebody was obviously a hunter. I shut down the car just as two big dogs – a German shepherd and a mastiff – bounded down the stairs from the deck and set up a fierce racket of welcome as they leapt up one after the other to snarl at me through the window. Fortunately the window was closed.

I sat there waiting, not about to risk my life by opening the door. After a few seconds I heard a yell and looked up to see a man at the top of the stairs. He shouted again, louder this time, and the dogs fell back and shut up. When it looked safe I opened the door and climbed out.

'Leland Whipple?' I asked, turning towards the man.

'Yeah, that's right. Can I help you?'

I glanced at his dogs.

'Wanted a word with you, if I could.' I closed the door and took a step towards the stairs. The mastiff growled deep in his throat. 'Are these guys safe?' I asked, frozen. 'They look like they're going to rip me apart.'

'They won't do that unless I tell them to,' Whipple said, smiling. 'Come on up.'

Trusting that he was telling the truth I ignored the dogs and climbed the stairs.

As expected, the view from the top was amazing, though the road below was concealed by trees. At one side of the deck was a barbecue made out of half of a steel drum on legs. A picnic table and two benches were positioned beside it. Hanging baskets dangling from brackets fixed to the trailer's walls on either side of the front door were filled with cascades of trailing petunias, geraniums and lobelia. A lady's touch, I reckoned. At the back of the deck there was a rough-boarded shack and a trail leading past it up the hill to another small shed with a stovepipe projecting through the roof. A column of white smoke wafted into the air above it, soon dissipating in the breeze from the sea.

'Smokehouse,' Whipple said, noticing the direction of my glance. 'Got some fish smoking – perch and ling cod.'

I nodded.

Whipple himself was short – about five-seven or so – and had a mane of thick black hair that fell almost to his shoulders. A good looking man behind his heavy rimmed glasses, he seemed to be in his late thirties or early forties. He was wearing jeans and a worn red plaid shirt with the sleeves rolled up, and he held a beer bottle in one hand. He also had a steel brace strapped to his lower left leg. I stepped toward him and held out my hand.

'Arnold Rednapp, Mr. Whipple. Connie and Muriel Walensky suggested I come out to see you. They gave me the directions.'

'The Walenskys are good people.' Whipple took my hand and shook it, his dark eyes burning into mine. 'What can I do for you?'

'I'm a reporter, sir. For a paper in the Bay area, the *South Bay Bulletin*. I'm up here looking into Leo Walensky's death. I understand you were one of his closest friends. I also understand you were one of the last people to see him alive.'

Whipple's face was an expressionless light mahogany mask.

'That's true,' he said. He looked about him, then squinted up at the sky. 'Going to get cool pretty soon, Mr. Rednapp, once the sun goes around that point. We could sit out here, but it might be more comfortable inside. Come on in and meet my wife.'

He led the way and I followed. As he walked his gammy leg made him roll from side to side. He was ambulatory, but no hurdle jumper. Which was why, I reckoned, he had to settle for a job as a school custodian.

He opened the trailer screen door and gestured me past him. I stepped inside. As I did, a slim white lady at the sink turned towards me, drying her hands on a worn hand towel. She looked early thirties, wore jeans and a pink tee-shirt, and had mousy blond hair gathered back in a loose ponytail.

'This is Mr. Rednapp, Ang,' Whipple told her, stepping in after me and closing the screen door. 'He's a newspaper reporter looking into Leo's death. The Walenskys sent him out here to talk to us.'

She dropped the towel over the back of a kitchen chair and stepped towards me.

'Mr. Rednapp?' she said, holding out her hand. I shook it. 'Pleased to meet you. Do you want coffee? Or would you prefer a beer?'

'A beer would be great,' I told her. 'And please, call me Arnie. Both of you.'

Whipple nodded.

'Okay, Arnie. I'm Lee. That's Angela. Ang for short. Let's sit down.'

While Whipple's wife got me a cold one from the fridge he led me around the breakfast counter and into a longish front room with windows that overlooked the parking area and the sea. The room was simply furnished and comfortable, with colorful hand-knitted afghan throws on the sofa back and armchairs and an ornate macramé sling hanging from a bracket beside the window holding a massive plant pot from which variegated ivy fell in leafy clusters towards the floor. Lee gestured toward the sofa and lowered himself into a recliner that faced the TV in the far corner. Another recliner sat beside it with a low table separating them. On the wall above them was a framed print of Landseer's 'Monarch of the Glen'. On other walls small pieces of Native American craftsmanship were displayed – antique beaded headbands and woven decorative pieces. On the coffee table before me a small, geometrically patterned reed basket held odds and ends. Beside it a cheap chess set was laid out, mid-game.

'Saw one of these already this afternoon,' I told Whipple, pointing at the set and smiling. 'On Leo Walensky's desk. Do you play chess, too?'

'Leo was teaching me.' He took a swig of his beer. 'I'm pretty crap at it, but he wouldn't give up. Said it was good for the mind.'

'His parents told me he was a fanatic about it. That and reading.'

Whipple nodded. 'He was. That's why he wouldn't give up on me. I told him he was wasting his time. The best he could get out of me was some lessons on how to hunt and catch fish.'

He smiled.

'How did you two become friends?' I asked him, after swigging at the beer Ang had handed me. It tasted good. She had sat down on the other recliner and was lighting a filter cigarette.

'We met at the elementary school,' Lee said. 'I'm caretaker there.'

'I know. The Walenskys told me. As it happens, I met Hazel Mendoza earlier today. Nice lady.'

Lee nodded. 'Yeah. Good boss, too. She hired me ten years ago.'

'Tell me about Leo,' I prompted, after another swig.

Lee shifted position in his chair, put his beer bottle down on the table at his side.

'Leo was always the lone kid on the playground. You couldn't help but notice him. At recesses and lunch times every year, while the other kids ... other boys ... were off horsing around or playing ball games he'd be amusing himself alone somewhere along the sidelines – playing with plastic figurines and talking to himself, or just sitting and reading. One day he noticed me working on some outdoor plumbing and hung around asking me questions.'

'What about?'

Lee shrugged.

'About me. About what I was doing. He had a great curiosity about everything and everyone. Wanted to know where I lived, how long I'd been doing this job. What it's like being Indian.'

'And you told him.'

'Told him what I could.' He gestured to the brace on his left leg. 'With me being crippled from polio as a kid I was never as deeply involved in tribal affairs as I could've been.' He looked at his wife, beside him. 'Then when I married Ang I made myself even more an outsider. Most of the older tribes-people don't like intermarriage. They want us to keep the Klamath blood pure.' He chuckled. 'A bit late for that. We lost that battle long ago – along with all the others. Anyway, after that whenever he saw me around he would stop to talk. We became friends.'

'How did you end up taking him fishing?'

'He asked me one Friday what I was doing over the weekend. I told him I was going surf fishing. He seemed interested so I asked him if he'd like to come along. He said yes, but that I'd have to talk to his folks about it. I did. They were surprised, but said they were happy for me to take him. Apparently they'd always had trouble getting him to do anything physical – other than riding his bike.' He smiled. 'Leo was twelve or thirteen then, starting to shoot up in height. But he was still small enough to have to struggle a bit with the fishing rod to hold it against the pull of the wave backwash.'

He stopped for a moment, remembering.

'Do you two have any kids?' I asked him.

He shook his head.

'No. We're still trying, but no luck so far.' He sighed. 'Maybe I'm crippled that way, too. Anyway, Leo and I fished for a couple hours that morning and he actually caught a few. Got really excited about it. I taught him how to clean the fish, and when we were through I took him home and he gave the fish to his mother to fry. He was really pleased with himself.'

'Must have improved his self-confidence a lot, I would imagine,' I offered.

'It did. Leo couldn't see very far in front of him. Only a few feet. So he couldn't see where he was dropping his hook when he cast out. He could only feel the pull of the receding water on the line, and – when it happened – the jerk of the bait being taken. He liked the fact that he didn't have to see that well to catch fish, and he got really excited every time he had one on the line.' Lee lifted his bottle and drained it, then sat back, holding it in his lap with two hands. 'The next time we went fishing together I brought him up here to meet Ang and to have lunch. Leo liked the place, and he obviously felt at home here, liked being with us. I told him he could come out anytime he felt like it, that he was always welcome. Over the years he became part of the family almost, dropping in several times a week and staying an hour or two every time.'

In her chair, Ang, who had sat listening without expression, nodded her head.

'He loved us. And we loved him, too.' She cleared her throat and shook herself slightly, tearing up. 'We'll miss him.'

I nodded, sympathetically.

'How did he get out here? Did you pick him up or did his parents bring him?'

'Mostly he rode his bicycle,' Lee said, placing his empty bottle on the side table. 'He rode that bike everywhere. Didn't want his parents to have to ferry him around in the car. He preferred to be independent. And even though his eyes were bad he did pretty well on that bike.'

I pulled my notebook and pen from my pocket.

'Do you mind if I make a few notes?'

They shook their heads.

'Not at all,' Lee responded. 'What else do you want to know?'

'Firstly,' I asked them, 'do you believe there was any possibility that Leo's death was suicide?'

Again immediate reactions from both – strong shakings of the head.

'No,' Lee said, flatly. 'Leo was in high spirits when I last saw him. It was no suicide.'

I nodded. 'Have you heard that his glasses were found at the top of the cliff?'

Lee looked to his wife, somber-faced. Then he looked back at me.

'Yeah, I heard that.'

'And that they couldn't find either his rucksack or his cell phone?'

He nodded.

'What do you make of that?' I asked him.

Whipple leant forward in his chair, resting his elbows on his knees. For a few seconds he stared at the floor. Then he looked up at me again.

'You probably know there's been some bad feeling in the town directed toward him over the last couple of months,' he said finally.

'Yes. I heard about the '*Humanist*' broadsheets he was putting in people's mailboxes. Do you think his death is somehow related to that?'

He shook his head slowly, frowning.

'It's hard to believe anyone would've killed him over that. it doesn't make sense.' He sat back again, clasping his hands in his lap. 'There are some bad ass people in this town, but even them ... I can't believe they'd do such a thing.' He shook his head again, defeated. 'No. It's a mystery. Something bad happened on that point, because Leo wouldn't have just walked off that cliff, especially without his glasses. He was too savvy. Somebody else must've been involved. But who or why I just don't know.'

I nodded. 'Lee, did you know he was responsible for the broadsheets?'

'Yes, I did.'

'Do you have any idea where he got them printed?'

'I do. At the school.' He looked at Ang, then at me. 'I did it for him. Three hundred copies each time. He provided the paper. I stayed an extra half hour after school and ran them off with the school printer. No one ever found out.'

I made a note.

'You won't tell anyone, will you?'

'Not unless it's necessary. And I can't imagine why that would be.'

He looked relieved.

'I don't want to lose my job.'

'You won't,' I assured him. 'What about the delivery of the broadsheets? Putting them in people's mailboxes? Did he do that alone, or did you help out with that, too?'

'I helped out. I'm not such a believer in these things as Leo was, but I could see the good sense it all made when he explained it to me, and I decided I'd do what I could to help him. Leo divided the town into three sections. He did the area around his place. I delivered to the section at the back of the town and out this way.'

I frowned. 'You said three sections. Who did the third one?'

I had hardly finished my question when the dogs set up another roar of welcome outside, dragging themselves heavily across the deck and down the stairs again to challenge someone else coming up the drive. Lee got to his feet and moved to the window, looking down.

'You're about to meet her,' he said. 'She's just driven in.'

Lee excused himself and went out to meet the new arrival, dropping his empty bottle off on the kitchen counter in passing. Ang also got to her feet, smiling at me nervously, and moved into the kitchen with her cigarette, grinding it out in an ashtray on the table. Then she emptied the ashtray into a garbage bin and stood at the screen door, waiting expectantly for Lee to return with the newcomer. As I rose and took a step or two towards her I could hear the distant murmur of their voices, their footsteps on the stairs, then crossing the deck. When they reached the door, Ang opened the screen and drew the visitor inside, gathering her into her arms in a firm hug. Lee came in behind them, pulling the screen to.

The two women stood holding one another for several seconds. Then the visitor stepped back and I could see her plainly.

She was young, about Leo's age – seventeen or eighteen. Blondish shoulder-length hair, attractive blue eyes set in a well-proportioned face. Quite a pretty girl in a quiet, unassuming way. She'd obviously been crying. She was wearing a white sweatshirt over jeans and had a nice figure. She looked at me with interest. Lee Whipple introduced us.

'Arnie Rednapp, meet Valerie Rush. Val, Arnie's a reporter from down south. He's here looking into Leo's death. He's come out to ask us some questions.'

The girl stepped forward, her head high, her step confident, her blue eyes fixed on mine.

'Pleased to meet you, Mr. Rednapp.'

'Please. Call me Arnie.'

We shook hands.

'Let's sit again,' Lee said. 'Want anything, Val? A coke? Some juice?'

She shook her head. 'No thanks. I'm good.'

The four of us sat down in the trailer's living room – the Whipples in their normal places, the girl and myself on either end of the sofa. When everyone was settled Lee filled her in on our progress.

'I've told him about the broadsheets, Val – that I printed them out and that the three of us did the delivering.'

She looked at me with a question in her eyes, but said nothing.

'Do you believe Leo killed himself, Valerie?' I asked her.

She shook her head. 'No.'

'Any idea what happened out there, then?'

She stared at me for a moment. Then she shook her head and looked down.

I eased myself a little in her direction.

'I don't want to distress you, Val. Do you mind talking about Leo?'

She looked up at me again, shook her head.

'I'm all right. Ask anything you like.'

'Okay. Firstly, do you share Leo's atheism and interest in Humanism?'

'Yes, I do. At least, I've come to. I was always kind of an agnostic – like him I couldn't bring myself to believe absolutely in something that couldn't be proven. Leo introduced me to Humanism, gave me some books to read. Gradually I came to think as he does ... did ... that only through discarding belief in divinities and living this life as if that's all there is can we ever find a way to exist together in true harmony.'

I nodded. Then frowned, remembering.

'Valerie Rush. Aren't you the girlfriend of Coach Anders' son, Bart?'

She shook her head.

'Not anymore. I broke up with him six months ago, when I found out he'd been seeing another girl – or girls – on the side. Also I was tired of his dope smoking.'

I raised my eyebrows.

'Dope smoking? Wow. I thought he was the hot-shot high school quarterback?'

'He is. Was. That's what makes it even worse.'

I produced my notepad again, bent to make a note, then glanced up at her.

'Do you mind?'

'Not at all.'

I finished writing my note, then looked up again.

'The Walenskys told me that you and Leo used to be friends as youngsters, but that you kind of drifted apart. Is that right?'

'Yes. We were a lot alike in our temperament and interests, and as kids we got on really well together. But as we grew older Leo became self-conscious about his handicap and his glasses. He started to be more private and aloof and seemed awkward around people – including me. So I made other friends. But I always liked him.'

'What drew you together again? And when did that happen?'

'I was out riding my bike one afternoon last spring and we met by accident. He was at a picnic spot just off the main road. He'd been out with his bike and had stopped to read for a while. I saw him and went over to say hello. We got to talking. He knew I'd broken off with Bart and said he was glad to hear that, that I'd been wasting my time on someone who was "unworthy of me".' She smiled. 'Those were his words, I remember. Anyway, the longer we talked the easier it felt to be with him – just like when we were little. When I left I gave him my cell number and told him to call me. He did, and we talked regularly after that, right up to ... to last week.'

'Did you often do things together?'

'If you mean did we date or anything the answer's no. I tried to keep my friendship with him a secret from everyone else and Leo was happy with that. Though we did meet sometimes at prearranged places – just to talk.'

'Why did you feel it necessary to keep your friendship a secret?'

She sighed deeply, and looked down at her hands.

'Bart has never really gotten over me leaving him, I think. He's still very jealous – makes a scene if I pay particular attention to anyone. Any boy, anyway. I thought that if we were open about our friendship Bart might do something to try to put Leo off.' She looked up at me. 'Bart's not bad, but he does have a temper. Sometimes he can get pretty ugly.'

I nodded, making a note. Possibilities were rambling around in my brain again.

'Do you think Bart found out about your renewed friendship with Leo and did do something about it?'

She looked at me a long time before speaking.

'No. I don't think he knew about us. And no, I don't think he had anything to do with ... with what happened. Bart's not that stupid. He wouldn't do anything so drastic.' She glanced at her watch and then at the Whipples. 'I've got to go. I told Mom I'd only stay a few minutes.' She turned briefly to me, then back to Whipple. 'Lee,' she continued, 'what're we going to do about the broadsheets? Are we going to deliver them, or what?'

Whipple stood up, put his hands in his pockets, thinking.

'What do you think we should do?'

Again Valerie Rush looked at me before answering.

'I think we should deliver them. I think that's what Leo would've wanted us to do. It was to be the last one anyway.'

Lee nodded. 'Okay. We'll do it tonight. Agreed?'

'Agreed.'

'I'd better do Leo's section,' Lee went on. 'His copies are lost, so I'll use mine to do his area. Some people won't get one, but that can't be helped.'

I made a connection.

'Wait a minute,' I said. 'Leo's copies were in his rucksack, weren't they? He was on his way home from your place after having picked them up that afternoon, wasn't he?'

Whipple nodded.

'That's right. He had a third of the copies. Around a hundred.'

I turned to Valerie.

'When did you pick up your copies?'

'That same afternoon. I came earlier. I left here with mine just as Leo got here. We met at the bottom of the drive, just as I was about to turn onto the road. We spoke for a couple minutes, but I had to get home and I told him to call me later. He never did.'

'Were you driving or on your bicycle?'

'I had Mom's car. Like today.'

I looked at Lee.

'What time did Leo leave here that afternoon?'

Lee glanced at his wife.

'What, about five? Five-thirty?'

'Yeah,' Ang said. 'Something like that. It was starting to get dark.'

'And he left here with the broadsheet copies in his rucksack?' I asked them.

'That's right.'

'And neither the rucksack nor his cell phone were recovered,' I said, thinking aloud.

'Yep.'

'I've got to go,' Valerie said, moving toward the door. 'Nice to meet you, Mr. Rednapp.'

'Arnie,' I said.

She smiled. 'Arnie. Call me if you need anything else.' She turned away and disappeared through the door. 'Lee has my cell number,' she called back as she hurried down the outside stairs with Lee close behind her.

'What do you think of Bart Anders, Lee?' I asked him after Valerie's car had left the drive and he had returned.

'Arrogant little bastard,' was Lee's immediate response. 'Could never understand what Val saw in him, other than his flash car and his jock status.'

'He has a flash car?'

'Yeah. A dark blue Audi TT convertible. Daddy bought it for him last year. Roars around these roads in it like we were a formula one racetrack. Anyway, Val's clear of him now so I don't care what he does anymore. Let him kill himself, if he wants.'

'Do you believe he could've had anything to do with Leo's death?' I asked, stepping towards the door.

'Naah,' he answered, following me. 'He talks big but he's really a coward. He wouldn't have the balls to do such a thing. Anyway, he didn't know anything about Leo and Val so there wouldn't be a motive. You'll see him around, I'm sure. Hangs with Scott Willis, the mayor's son. Both of them are dorks.'

I hesitated by the door and looked back.

'Do you think Leo and Val were starting to get it together as a couple?'

Lee pursed his mouth.

'Maybe. They'd become good friends again, anyway. Who knows what the future would've brought.'

'Who knows indeed,' I concluded.

I asked Lee for Val's cell number, which I wrote in my notebook. Then I put the notebook and pen away, shook both Lee and Ang's hands and thanked them for the beer and their help. Lee walked with me to the head of the deck steps, watched me descend.

'You know,' he said behind me, 'if I thought that little bastard did have anything to do with Leo's death I think I could kill him myself.'

I stopped and turned back. I'd seen the rack of lethal looking rifles in the hall. Lee was obviously a hunter as well as a fisherman, and probably a good one.

'Yeah,' I said. 'I understand your feelings, Lee. But that wouldn't be a good idea even if he was guilty.'

'Maybe not.' He smiled. 'But it might make me feel better.'

'I'm staying at 'The Tides',' I told him. 'If you think of anything else.'

'If I do, I'll contact you. Look after yourself, now,' he ended with a wave, turning away.

The dogs paid me no mind this time. I guess I was regarded as family now.

Just as Leo had been.

5.

The sun was low in the sky and shadows were long as I swung the Cobalt onto the narrow county road back towards town. There were a few tourist cars parked along the beach side of the road – people out walking on the sand, looking for shells and interesting bits of driftwood, watching the evening drawing in. Already there were tinges of red in the west and the sunset promised to be another corker.

I was gunning the engine up the slope beyond the beach, arranging in my mind my schedule for the following day, when I shot past the vista point turnout and noticed a flash of color in the car park. A shiny dark blue convertible, with its top down.

Fifty yards past the turnout I slowed the Cobalt and pulled off to stop on the shoulder.

Lee had just told me about a blue sports car. An Audi TT convertible.

Bart Anders' car.

I wasn't sure that was it, but it'd be a strange coincidence if it was any other blue convertible parked there at this time of the afternoon.

I switched off the engine and climbed out.

There was a thick stand of fir trees bordering the road on both sides at this point and I couldn't see the parking area until I'd walked back twenty-five yards or so. As the vista point turnout came into view I stepped into the screen of trees at the edge of the road and continued forward more slowly. I'd only moved a few feet when I saw the rounded back end of the car and heard strains of country rock music and the indistinct murmur of voices. I knew the music – the Dixie Chicks' anti-Iraq-war song '*Truth No. 2*'. Whoever they were I approved of their taste.

Suddenly a young man popped into view behind and beyond the car. He was in tee-shirt and jeans, with a head of unruly dark hair, and seemed to be searching for something along the metal railing that separated pavement from brush and cliff edge. A second later another figure appeared, similarly dressed, with a close-cropped blond crew-cut. This second guy was cupping in his right hand what looked to be a lit spliff. While the first boy searched, this one just looked on, taking an occasional puff of weed while glancing about nervously. I crept closer, making sure there was a screen of tree trunks and brush between me and them. Finally I could make out what they were saying.

'It ain't here, Bart,' said the searcher. 'I've looked all along where it might've been caught, but it's gone if it ever was here.' He straightened and turned back toward his companion. 'I reckon it got blown out to sea.'

'You better hope it did,' the other boy told him. He took a long pull on his joint and held it out towards his friend. 'Want a hit on this?'

'Nah,' the first boy said. 'Come on. Let's get out of here. Place gives me the creeps.'

Crew-cut took a final puff on the roach, then dropped it onto the asphalt and ground it to bits with the toe of his shoe. I watched as the two boys moved to climb back into their car, then stepped briskly back to mine. I was standing at the driver's door with my hand on the handle when the blue Audi backed out into the road and sped towards me. As it drew near, the driver slowed and the vehicle moved past almost at idle speed. Both boys' faces were fixed on mine. Both were frowning. I looked back at them without expression.

Then the car roared away, peeling rubber.

I climbed into the Cobalt and drove off after them, wondering what it was they'd been seeking. A rucksack? A cell phone? A crumpled handbill?

Maybe something that had nothing to do with Leo, or his unfortunate demise.

Anybody that liked the Dixie Chicks couldn't be all bad, and I refused to jump to any conclusions about what they'd been up to until I'd learned more about young Bart Anders and his friend.

Then we'd see.

Back at the motel I had three calls to make: one to my daughter Lisa back in Iowa; the second to Lorraine, the alluring waitress from the Cove; the last to Guy Abbott, the English teacher/chess champion who had been Leo Walensky's mentor. I decided I'd wait to give Abe Rawlings an update till I had more to tell him.

The first two calls were a breeze.

Lisa was glad to hear from me, said her flight had been uneventful and that now she was just chilling out with her friends before school started in a few days. I told her where I was, what I was doing, and that I'd call her again when I got home to the city. We blew kisses down the phone and hung up. Ten minutes total from beginning to end.

My call to Lorraine took even less time. I asked her if she wanted to come out for dinner with me that evening – maybe drive into Fortuna or somewhere for a change of scene? She countered by offering to make me a seafood dinner at her place, with a nice chilled bottle of Chablis to go with it. Sounded great to me so I agreed to be there at 8:00, promising to bring a second bottle of wine with me – in case the seafood made us thirsty. She laughed, gave me her address and told me how to find it. Then we hung up.

Finally I called Guy Abbott on the number Mr. Walensky had given me. The phone rang four or five times before it was picked up.

'Yes? Guy Abbott here?'

My first surprise. Guy Abbott had an English accent – worn down a bit over time, but still distinctly there. A touch of the cut glass. Also slightly effete, reminding me of old recordings of Noel Coward.

'Mr. Abbott, my name is Arnold Rednapp,' I told him. 'I'm a reporter from the *South Bay Bulletin* in South San Francisco, and I've been sent up here to look into the tragic death of young Leo Walensky. I gather he was a student of yours, and that you often played chess together?'

'That's right, Mr. Rednapp. Leo was a very gifted player and a fine student. He was also my friend. I shall miss him. We'll all miss him.'

'Of course,' I offered, lamely.

'What can I do for you, Mr. Rednapp?'

'Leo's parents, Connie and Muriel Walensky, suggested that it would be useful for me to meet you, to discuss your friendship with their son. They said you could fill me in on the kind of young man he was, and might have some idea as to why he ended up as he did.'

'As to the latter,' Abbott countered, 'I cannot help you at all. I really have no idea why a bright boy like Leo would either want to take his own life, or be stupid enough to walk out near a cliff edge when his eyesight was so poor. No, I'm afraid the whole thing is just a very tragic mystery to me, Mr. Rednapp. All the same, I'm happy to meet with you to discuss our chess games – Leo's and mine – if that will be of any help.'

'I'd appreciate it,' I told him. 'Are you free tomorrow about noon? I'm in Shelter Cove, but I can drive over to be there by then. How about I take you out to lunch? Your wife, too, if she's free.'

'That'd be very nice, Mr. Rednapp, but alas there's no wife. I'm a widower. Been on my own now for some years.'

Ooops.

'Sorry to hear that, Mr. Abbott.'

'No need to be. You couldn't have known. Do you have my address?'

'I do. The Walenskys gave it to me.'

Abbott described how to find his street from the Fortuna main drag and suggested a cafe downtown that did great sandwiches and soup. Sounded fine to me. I told him I'd pick him up around 12:15, thanked him for agreeing to see me and hung up.

I had a rest for an hour or so, then took a shower and changed into a fresh light blue shirt and tan slacks. By 7:30 the dusk was firmly advanced, and the sky colors filtering through my window bathed the floor and walls in a faintly rosy hue. I brushed my teeth, combed my hair again, grabbed my jacket and headed out to the car to make for the Shelter Cove General Store to purchase of a bottle of good vintage red.

The store was busy. Among the dozen or so vehicles parked out front were two or three king-cab pickups pulling aluminum johnboats behind them on trailers. Out for the day fishing from the cove, obviously. I went inside. For such a moderate sized establishment the general store had a wide range of merchandise – everything from building materials and hardware to food basics, from clothes to fishing gear, guns and ammunition. What's more, there was an excellent selection of wines, which – given the alleged wealth of some of the residents – probably wasn't so surprising. I chose a bottle of full-bodied Merlot that I was partial to, grabbed a small box of Lindt chocolates on a sudden impulse, then stood in line at the till, waiting while a tired-looking lady in a '49ers sweatshirt served a half-dozen people. Finally she got to me. When she'd finished checking the items I paid her and took my change, gathered my purchases together in a paper bag and headed outside.

I had just dumped my stuff in the car's back seat and was preparing to climb in when Deputy Williams' green and white 4 x 4 county cruiser pulled into the parking slot beside me. I waited while he dismounted from his rig and walked around to the front of mine.

He was in civvies – light jacket over a yellow golf shirt and jeans.

''Evening, Deputy,' I opened. 'Stopping for a bag of sugar, or did you just see me and want to have a chat?'

He grinned, held out what looked to be a shopping list.

'Orders from the wife. But no sugar this time.'

I moved up to shake his hand.

'Day off today?'

'Yeah,' he said. 'Sundays are usually off for me. Been down at Benbow, playing eighteen holes with Dale Anders. Just got back.'

The Benbow Inn was south on 101, a large '30s resort and hotel with adjoining golf course. Apparently it'd been a favorite vacation retreat for John Barrymore back in the day. I'd passed it on the way up.

I looked out at the fading sunset.

'Right weather for it.'

'Sure was.' He stepped closer, looked around. There was no one near us. 'How's the investigation going?' he asked, quietly.

'Rolling on. Slowly putting together a picture. When I have all the pieces assembled I'll let you know.'

He nodded. 'You around tomorrow?'

'Most of the time. Going in to Fortuna to see a former teacher of Leo's. Man named Guy Abbott. Know him?' Williams shook his head. 'Why did you want to know if I'm around tomorrow?'

'Thought we might get together at some point. Compare notes.'

'Any word yet on that blood smudge?'

He moved his mouth.

'We'd need a DNA test to be sure, but it's quite likely Leo Walensky's blood. He had the rarest blood type, AB negative. The blood on that broadsheet is AB negative.'

'And you don't think that's suspicious?'

'Getting to be. Thought I'd talk things over with you first, though, before I take this thing to Sheriff Dunlap. Far as he's concerned the case is closed. He won't be happy reopening it unless I have some hard evidence to show him.'

'Fair enough,' I said. 'I'll be around tomorrow afternoon. Maybe we can get together then?'

'Sounds good. I'll look you up.'

'Want my cell number?'

He shook his head.

'Got it already. Anyway, I know where you're staying. There's no hurry on this. I'll catch up with you sooner or later.'

'Right.' I glanced at my watch. 'Gotta go, Deputy. Hot date.'

He raised his eyebrows. 'You're a fast worker.'

'Nope. Dinner invitation from a kind local citizen. I'm a sucker for home cooking.'

'Well, enjoy,' he said, grinning and backing away. 'See you tomorrow.'

I watched him pass into the store and disappear.

Then I fired up the Cobalt.

Lorraine Adams (she'd written her full name on the map to the Walenskys' place) lived in a small modern house not far from the restaurant – within easy walking distance in fact, which must have saved her gas money. When I saw how close it was I drove back to the motel, parked my car in front of my room and walked back to her house carrying the paper bag. Might as well avoid any chance of being caught DUI later on the way home.

There was a white VW Polo parked in her driveway. I walked up the cement pathway towards the front entrance. A neighbor was mowing his lawn next door in the waning light. He looked up at me and smiled. I nodded and smiled back.

Lorraine had the door open when I reached her porch. She pushed open the screen for me and stepped back to let me enter.

'Come on in, handsome. You're right on time.'

'Bad habit of mine,' I told her. 'Too used to living with deadlines.'

74

I stepped past her into a short hallway that gave immediately into a modest living room with comfortable furniture.

Lorraine was wearing a sleeveless white blouse with a couple of the top buttons undone, and a pair of tight, black levis. She looked good. Her hair, which in the restaurant was always gathered at the back of her head with some kind of a clasp, was loose now, and fell over her shoulders in a honey-hued cascade, making her look younger than her years and very attractive.

She shut the front door and followed me into the living room.

'Drink?'

'Glass of that Chablis you mentioned, if that's okay with you, gorgeous.' I took the bottle of red I'd purchased from the bag and held it out to her. 'This is for later. If we get to later.' She smiled and took it. Then I dug out the box of chocolates. Her eyebrows raised as she accepted them. 'Present for a nice lady.'

'Thanks. The nice lady might get even nicer if you carry on treating her like this.'

I smiled. 'Then it's all been worth it.'

She motioned towards the sofa and chairs.

'Sit anywhere you like. I'll get our drinks. Dinner in half an hour.'

She moved off towards the kitchen and I sat down on the sofa, looking around at her space. It was obviously a house without a male presence for everything was neat and tidy and arranged with care and attention to attractiveness as well as comfort. There were a few teenager celebrity magazines stacked on a coffee table together with the latest issue of *Cosmopolitan*. The TV sat on a low table in a corner, with stacks of DVDs laid out beside it. The pictures on the wall were mostly framed prints of French masters – a Renoir, a Matisse. A Paul Klee was the exception. On a sideboard on one wall, beside a vase of fresh flowers centered on a white crocheted doily, a series of framed photographs were ranged in an echelon. The largest of these was of a young girl, probably Lorraine's daughter (Mandy?), smiling happily down from the back of a horse. Two or three other pictures featured her either with her mother or friends or relatives. In one she stood arm in arm with a tall, thin man in a suit. The similarity of facial features and expression told me that this was her father, Lorraine's ex. He looked a nice enough fellow. Kind eyes, good head of hair, gentle smile. Two attractive people, he and Lorraine. I wondered what had happened?

Lorraine came back with two glasses of Chablis, gave me one, and took the other with her to sit in an armchair at my right. I shifted my body in her direction and smiled.

'So,' she said, lifting her glass towards me. 'Here's to us!'

'And to long life and good health,' I appended, reaching out to touch my glass to hers.

We drank, then sat back in our places, getting comfortable, smiling across at one another. From off in the kitchen I could hear faint strains of classical piano music – Rachmaninoff or someone similar. Just at the right level.

'Nice music,' I told her.

'Thanks. It's a CD. I like to listen to classical while I'm cooking.' She took a sip of wine. 'We're having sea bass. I hope you like fish?'

'I love fish. Sea bass especially.'

'Good,' she said, smiling. 'Then my instincts were right about that, too.'

Lorraine's instincts were spot on, as the Brits say, and the evening as it rolled out was relaxed and very pleasant indeed. The meal – which we took sitting opposite one another at a small, attractively laid out table on the shallow deck at the back of the house – was delicious and went to four courses, concluding with coffee and brandy taken with chocolates offered from her opened box of Lindts. By the time we'd finished a pale crescent moon peeked out from behind distant fir trees. Between us on the tablecloth two fat candles cast a warm glow over our faces. Her face looked good in the candlelight. I was liking it more and more.

By then we had pretty much talked out the basics of both our lives and had come as a result to feel even more comfortable together. I'd believed I was in no way open to another long-standing relationship, but I had to admit that if I had been Lorraine would've been a prime candidate.

As we entered our third shared hour the need to speak began to taper off, and we found ourselves just sitting back and enjoying the night and the music wafting through the back door from the kitchen. Then the CD ended, and there was left only the soughing of the distant surf.

I lifted my glass, drained the last of the red wine. Lorraine had finished hers a few moments before. It was time for a change of scene.

'This has been wonderful, Lorraine,' I told her, 'but how about we take a walk down by the sea? Maybe stop in for a nightcap somewhere?'

'I'd like that,' she said, then smiled coyly back at me. 'As long as you see me back home afterwards, mister. A girl can't be too careful, you know?'

'That was always my plan,' I assured her.

We doused the candles and turned on some lights, and I helped her clear the dishes back to the kitchen, and to rinse them and stack them in the dishwasher. Wonderful thing, modern technology. Then she grabbed a cardigan and pulled it round her shoulders, and I picked up my jacket, and off we set toward the cove and the beach beyond. Once there, sauntering slowly over the packed sand at the surf's edge in the thin moonlight, I felt her hand reach out to take mine.

'Do you mind?' she asked.

'Not at all.' I squeezed her fingers.

We walked on, like two high school sweethearts after the prom.

'How are you doing with your investigation?' Lorraine asked after a time. 'Found your story yet? Or is that confidential?'

'No, it's not confidential. I've talked with several people who've been helpful, but I haven't made much headway. There's still reason to believe the boy's death was suspicious, though I haven't found any real evidence yet of anything untoward. Maybe there's nothing. I'll hang around a day or two more. Hopefully things will become a bit clearer by then.'

She released my hand and took my arm instead, snuggling herself against me in the night.

'Well,' she said, huskily. 'I'm sorry you've not found what you're looking for, Arnie. But I can't say I'm unhappy about you having to stay a day or two longer. I kinda like having you here.'

I squeezed her arm against my side.

'I kinda like being here, Lorraine.'

Twenty minutes later we were sitting in a booth in the Cove Lounge, which sat at the side of the restaurant. It was quiet, with only one other couple in another booth and a lone local in a baseball cap nursing a beer at the bar. When the bartender had broken off talking to him and come over, smiling and winking familiarly at Lorraine, I had ordered a JD on the rocks, and Lorraine a glass of port. Now we sat working on our drinks, enjoying the ambiance and one another.

Lorraine launched into a relaxed monologue about her daughter, Mandy, telling me how proud she was of her, how she thought she was going to do well in life. Then without any prompting she told me more about the dissolution of her marriage. Her ex-husband, Ted, was a tax accountant, a workaholic employed by Apple in L.A. who had ended up spending more and more time away from home. Finally the marriage had just come apart at the seams, like a badly-made garment. They were still friends, she told me, but the romance was gone. I asked her if she missed it.

'Not with him,' she said, and smiled.

We were just about to drink up and go home when Dale Anders came into the Lounge from the restaurant, glanced around and saw us, then walked on to have a quiet word with the bartender, who was drying glasses behind the bar. Then Anders turned and ambled across to our booth, a smug half smile on his face.

''Evening, Lorraine. Mr. Rednapp.'

Lorraine smiled nervously up at him.

'Coach Anders,' I returned.

'Nice to see you're getting on with the locals, Mr. Rednapp. That might prove to you what I said is true – that Shelter Cove residents aren't bad people.'

'I never thought they were,' I told him. I sipped my JD. 'I gather you had a good day at Benbow today. Did you win?'

He crossed his arms, staring down at me. It obviously irked him that I knew what he'd been doing.

'I did, as a matter of fact. Finished eighteen holes with a 68 – two under par with a three stroke handicap. Not bad for an amateur. You a golfer?'

I shook my head.

He nodded, his eyes still on mine.

'How're you getting on with your ... enquiries?' he asked finally.

I shrugged. 'Step by step, Mr. Anders. No great discoveries yet.'

'You will come to me if you do find anything, won't you?'

'I told you I would.'

He looked at me for a long moment without speaking. Then he dropped his folded arms and held out his hand.

'Well, good luck to you.'

I took the hand and shook it.

'Thanks.'

'You two have a good night now, y'hear?' He glanced from Lorraine to me with a wry smile.

Then he turned and walked out.

As promised, I walked Lorraine home. I was going to give her a hug and a kiss on the cheek on her doorstep and leave her in peace, but she wouldn't let me get away with that. Instead she took my face in her two hands and kissed me on the mouth, slowly and thoroughly, pressing her softly rounded body into me.

There was no fighting her, even if I wanted to.

I didn't want to.

It was daybreak when I finally got back to the motel. When I did I found a folded paper stuck under one of the Cobalt's windshield wipers. I took it into my room. Switching on the light, I unfolded the paper and sat down on my bed to read it. It was an ordinary piece of lined notebook paper, but the message it contained was made up of individual letters cut from printed matter and pasted into rough lines. Some of the colored letters seemed familiar, and I recalled seeing stacks of tourist brochures beside the cash register at the restaurant, and in a rack in the motel office. Clearly they were available all over town and anyone could have picked them up from anywhere. The letters almost certainly came from those brochures.

The message? Short and direct.

'*Listen, Frisco faggot, no one wants you here. Poke your nose too far into other people's business and you might get it snipped off. You've been warned.*'

I folded the note up again, stuck it into my jacket pocket and went to bed.

6.

When I roused myself from sleep later that morning warm sun was streaming through the gap in my curtains again and there were sounds of activity outside – murmuring voices, car doors slamming, distant traffic. For a few moments I lay on my back, enjoying the warmth of the bed and the memories of the night before. It was good that I was due to go home soon. I was beginning to think about that lady far too often.

By 11:00 I had showered and dressed and was sitting in my usual booth at the Cove, enjoying the bear claw and coffee that Lorraine had just brought me. I was pleased to see that our shared night had not changed the way we behaved towards one another. Still flirty and jokey and off-hand. No heavy undertones. I wondered how long that would last.

A couple minutes later she returned holding a single sheet of printed paper.

'This was in my mailbox this morning,' she said. 'Thought you might want to see it.'

She handed it to me. It was a copy of the last broadsheet Leo Walensky had written, the same issue that I had found balled up at the vista point. Obviously Lee and Val had made their deliveries as intended.

'Thanks,' I told Lorraine. 'Did you read it?'

'Yes, I did. Not exactly my thing, but I agree with the sentiments right enough. You can keep that,' she said, nodding toward the page. 'I don't want it.'

'I will,' I said, laying it aside. 'You're an angel.'

I would put it with the others in the plastic sleeve – in case the Walenskys didn't get one this time.

I told Lorraine that I'd phone her in the afternoon, and she countered by suggesting that perhaps tonight she'd allow me to treat her to dinner at one of the other local restaurants. Then she'd left me in peace with my coffee and pastry.

By 11:30 I was in the car on my way to Fortuna, retracing my steps up the winding road that joined highway 101 inland. When I reached the junction at Garberville twenty minutes later I turned north and cruised along the four-lane in light traffic along the Eel River and through the massive stands of redwoods till the forested hills dissolved into a broad coastal plain and I reached the first Fortuna turn-off, where I slowed and looped around to join the local roads.

Fortuna was obviously an old town of some ten to fifteen thousand inhabitants, with broad streets and scores of well-preserved Victorian gingerbread houses and storefronts. I passed a baseball diamond and football field alongside a collection of modern buildings with a sign outside that read 'Fortuna Union High School.' This must have been where Leo had spent his last years before graduating. Further along on the main drag fading posters still advertised the Fortuna Rodeo that had been held there during July. I had never seen a rodeo – at least not a proper one out west – and was sorry my visit hadn't coincided with the rodeo dates. Maybe another time.

My watch read 12:15 exactly when I pulled the Cobalt to a halt at the address for Guy Abbot that had been given me by the Walenskys – a modest, single-story grey clapboard house on a side street not far from the town center. The '20s house was set close to the road, only ten or fifteen feet off it, with a picket fence at the front surrounding a postage-stamp lawn bordered by bushes in need of pruning. The front porch, which extended the full width of the house, was entirely closed in by screens. Behind these, as I saw while approaching the porch door, a couple of ancient wooden armchairs sat together on one side and an old-fashioned two-person swing seat on the other, suspended from hooks in the ceiling. A few pot plants rested on saucers on the rail behind the screen. They looked well-tended. The porch door screen was closed so I stopped there and knocked on the door frame. A few seconds later the glazed front door beyond was opened and a middle-aged man in a long-sleeved light blue shirt, dark grey slacks with suspenders and a wine-red bow tie stepped out to open the porch door for me. He looked a bit like an aging Peter Ustinov, with less hair.

'Mr. Abbott?' I asked.

'That's right,' he said, extending his hand, which I shook. Then he stepped back to let me pass. 'Come on in, Mr. Rednapp. I'll just grab a jacket and we can go.'

The house inside was much as I would have expected for an older man living alone, though he obviously either hired a housekeeper or did the cleaning himself regularly for the place was neat as a pin and dust free. He was also, clearly, a nonsmoker. Being an older house, there was a lot of dark wood paneling here and there, leaving the ambient light dim and the atmosphere cool and a bit musty, but I felt immediately at home in the place. Tall filled bookcases were scattered around everywhere, and in one corner a large oak desk took up a good part of one wall. A swiveling captain's chair parked in front of it seemed to be the commanding position in the room. Across from it in another corner a heavy stuffed armchair faced the smallish television positioned near the front door, a worn leather chesterfield below the front windows taking up the rest of the wall space, together with an antique chiffonier opposite it, with framed photographs ranged across its top. On a small oriental table at one side of the armchair a set of carved ivory and onyx chess pieces were laid out in mid-game positions on an inlaid oak and mahogany chessboard. It looked the same game layout as the one I'd seen in Leo's room. I wondered if it was one they'd been playing at long distance before he'd died.

'I'll be just a minute,' he said, as he stepped away toward the back of the house down a short hallway. 'Make yourself at home.'

'Thanks,' I said.

I wandered over to look at the framed photographs, most of which were black and white images taken years ago.

In several of them a younger version of Guy Abbott appeared with various friends and relatives – the earliest photos clearly taken in England. In one of these he was dressed in black gown and mortarboard, smiling and holding a rolled diploma of some sort in front of an impressive and slightly familiar stone building. Oxford? Cambridge? Then there was a series of photos in which he appeared arm in arm with a young woman with light, slightly curly short hair. Then a wedding picture of the two of them, posing together with family and friends in front of a village church. Other pictures celebrated shared holiday adventures as the pair grew older together and explored various exotic corners of the world. At the center of the photo display, standing at the back of the chiffonier, in pride of place and clearly much favored, a larger silver-framed color picture of the woman smiled out, now with greying hair and lively blue eyes. A fairly recent photo, I reckoned, for here she looked to be in her mid-fifties or early sixties. I guessed Abbott, from what I had seen thus far, to be in his mid-sixties. I was still studying the woman's face when Abbott himself reappeared at my shoulder wearing a brown tweed jacket with leather elbow patches.

'That was Maddie,' he told me, his voice quiet. 'My dear wife of nearly forty years. She died five years ago, of a brain tumor.' He sighed. 'I miss her terribly.'

'I'm so sorry,' I said. I turned to him. 'You have no children?'

He shook his head, slipping his hands into his trouser pockets.

'Alas, no. We would've liked to have had children, but it just wasn't to be.' He sighed. 'Something wrong with my plumbing, apparently. So I've had to let my students and my teaching fill the gap they would have taken up in my life.' He tilted his head to one side. 'All in all, that has been enough for me. I've been pretty lucky, really.' He smiled. 'Shall we go?'

The cafe Abbott had recommended was on one of Fortuna's central main streets, an old-fashioned place that looked like a soda fountain out of the '*Our Town*' period of early Americana, with a marble-topped counter across the back of the room, white tile halfway up the walls, and wooden booths along one side and at the front. When we walked in the girls serving at the back made a big deal of welcoming 'Mr. Abbott', who seemed to enjoy the attention. Both of them were probably old students of his. They directed us to his 'usual' booth in the front window and we sat and – on his recommendation – ordered BLTs and a bowl of homemade soup, which today was spicy tomato. We each asked for coffee, and one of the young waitresses was back a second later with two mugs and a glass coffee pot. When she had done the honors we were left to await our sandwiches in peace.

'You're from England,' I opened, when she'd gone.

'That's right. From Horsham in West Sussex. But I've been in America almost forty years. I carry both passports now.'

'I noticed the picture of you with the gown and mortarboard. Oxford? Or Cambridge?'

He smiled.

'Neither. Durham. A good university. I read English and Philosophy there, back when dinosaurs still roamed the woods. Then I came to America to do a Masters Degree at San Francisco State. Met Maddie there.'

'She was American?'

'No. Oddly enough she was Welsh. She'd done her BSc in

Biology in Cardiff and had decided, like me, to do her graduate work in America. It was a wise decision. San Francisco State was, and remains, an excellent university. Maddie and I met and fell in love during our first year there. We were enjoying America, and when we finished our degrees we both applied for visas to remain as high school teachers – she in life sciences, me in English. Because there was a teacher shortage we were both accepted. With that settled we decided to get married, which we did on a quick return trip to Britain. Ten years later we went through the naturalization process and became dual nationals. And that was that.'

'Do you go back to England often?'

'Used to. When Maddie was alive we'd spend a few weeks there every summer. Even bought a little cottage on the south coast, near Dover, to retire into when the time came. I still have it.' He took a sip of his coffee. 'This will be my last year of teaching. I turn 65 in November and in the State of California that's the mandatory retirement age for teachers. Like it or not I shall be out of a job next summer, so I thought I might sell up then and take Maddie's ashes back home to be interred.'

'Do you still have friends there?'

'Some. And relatives. The cottage is in a little place called St. Margaret's Bay in Kent, just at the eastern end of the white cliffs. Lovely spot. I'm thinking it'd be a nice place to end up.'

The waitress appeared with our orders and for the next few minutes nothing much was said. When we had finished, however, and the plates had been cleared and our cups refilled with steaming coffee, Abbott turned to business.

'So, Mr. Rednapp,' he said, settling back on his maroon vinyl banquette and crossing his arms. 'What can I do for you?'

'You can tell me about Leo Walensky,' I said. 'His parents said you were a huge influence on him, that he read pretty much every book you ever mentioned to him. Also that it was you who fired up his chess ambitions, turned him from a good player into a young man who could have entered competitions.'

Abbott raised his eyebrows.

'Competitions? Well, we never talked about that, but I suppose he might have done. He did learn very fast, and was beginning to give even me a hard time.' He looked momentarily embarrassed. 'Sorry. I should say that I was a regional chess champion in my youth back in England. These days, though, I only play for fun.'

'Was it you who introduced him to Humanism?'

'Yes. In my Senior English class I include discussions about various contemporary philosophies and religions, giving the students interesting topics to write about in their essays. Something challenging for young minds, you understand?'

'Are you a Humanist yourself?'

He pursed his mouth, thinking.

'I suppose I'm that if I'm anything. I've never really liked joining groups, Mr. Rednapp. Let's just say that I have a great sympathy for the basic tenets of Humanism.'

'Are you an atheist?'

'Oh, yes.'

'Forgive me for asking, sir,' I said, dropping my voice slightly, 'but were you responsible in any way for Leo's atheism?'

He smiled, shook his head.

'Young Leo had turned away from a belief in God long before I met him. That was one of the things that drew us so closely together – we shared so many similar views on politics and philosophy. Leo had a very keen mind, Mr. Rednapp – he was mature well beyond his years. He loved the world of ideas, hated small-mindedness and the prejudice born of ignorance and complacency.'

'So I understand.' I lifted the plastic sleeve of Leo's broadsheets that I had brought from the car and withdrew the sheaf of papers. 'You've seen these?' I asked him, passing them over.

Guy Abbott took the pages and rested them on the table before him while he produced a pair of spectacles from his pocket and balanced them on his nose. Then he studied the pages carefully, skimming each one with a keen eye as he worked through them. Finally he shuffled them together and handed them back to me, putting his spectacles away again.

'No,' he said, as I replaced the pages in the plastic holder. 'I haven't seen them before, Mr. Rednapp. But I can tell who wrote them. Where did you get them and what are they?'

I filled him in on the story of Leo's mission, describing the manner in which the broadsheets were secretly written, printed and disseminated. As I spoke, Abbott's eyes twinkled with an ever greater amusement.

'Blimey!' he said when I had finished. 'No, Mr. Rednapp, I knew nothing of any of this. Leo certainly never mentioned his little campaign to me. But it doesn't surprise me. We did talk often of the suffering and hardship fundamentalist religious beliefs have brought to this world. Like him, I believe that humanity's only hope for survival rests in turning our backs on religion altogether.' He sighed, raised his eyebrows. 'But I have little faith that will ever happen. Mankind is too enamoured of its crutches.' He looked at me again and smiled. 'Leo still thought it was possible, however. He was young. His youthful optimism hadn't yet had time to be ground down to the cynical despair of maturity.'

I took a sip of coffee, looking for a change of topic to something more useful and less depressing.

'What was Leo like, Mr. Abbott? Did he have many friends? Did people like him?'

'Leo was not a popular lad,' he returned after a moment's thought, 'but he was certainly well-respected. Even liked, in a distant, impartial kind of way. People sympathized with him over his eye problems, but apart from that, he was pretty much a loner and his peers left him to get on with it. Of course, all of the staff got on well with him. It isn't often, Mr. Rednapp, that a teacher is gifted with a pupil that hungry to learn.'

'What about Coach Anders? Did he like Leo, too?'

Abbott made a face.

'Leo had no interest in athletics, which immediately put him at odds with Dale. I gather he gave Leo a rough time occasionally during P.E. classes, but I don't think he actually disliked him. Just found him a bit of a strange fish.'

I nodded.

'To your knowledge did Leo have any friends in the school?'

He shook his head.

'Apart from me, no. None that I knew of, at least. He was very self-contained.'

'I understand he sometimes stayed after school, and that you and he played chess together until he got the late afternoon bus home.'

'That's right. We played either in the school library, or here, or in a little tea shop on the other side of the street down towards the high school. If the weather was fine we sometimes sat outside at a picnic table in the park. We'd play for an hour or so, then he'd go. I had nothing else to do, no one to go home to. I enjoyed our games. I shall miss them.'

I nodded.

'Do you think he took his own life, Mr. Abbott?'

'Certainly not,' he returned, flatly. 'Leo was eager to start at Stanford. He was counting the days. There was absolutely no reason for him to kill himself.'

'Do you know Valerie Rush, sir?' I asked him.

That question seemed to surprise him, and he took a moment before answering.

'Of course I do. Valerie is another bright spark, valedictorian of her year. Off to San Jose State soon to read biochemistry, I believe. Why do you ask?'

'I understand Leo and she had become close friends over the last couple of months. You obviously were not aware of that?'

He looked blank.

'Not at all. They were alike in some ways, but to my knowledge Val never showed any particular fondness for him. In fact, it's my understanding that she's the girlfriend of a popular football player, Bart Anders. Strange choice for her – a bit of a rough character, Anders, for my money. But no. If there was any kind of special friendship between Valerie and Leo I certainly was never aware of it.'

I nodded.

'I met Val yesterday,' I told him. 'Nice girl. She told me she had split up with Bart Anders a few months ago. What kind of kid is he, Mr. Abbott? I met his father in Shelter Cove. Can you tell me anything about the son?'

Abbott looked down at the table top, ran his forefinger along the Formica's edge.

'To be honest, I hardly knew him. Oh, he was in one or two of my classes over the years and did well enough – low 'B' grade average as I remember – but he was hardly my kind of fellow. Too loud and cocky for my taste. But certainly popular. The young ladies found him very desirable. Even Valerie Rush, obviously. But I'm glad she's dropped him. Not in her class at all.'

I smiled.

'That's what Leo thought. He told Val Anders was "not worthy" of her.'

'Did he now?' Abbott said, tickled. 'How amusing.'

I changed gears.

'Mr. Abbott, do you think Bart Anders could be dangerous? Did he have a bad side, a violent temper, any sign that he might be capable of cruelty or inflicting real harm on someone else?'

Abbott thought for a moment.

'He had a temper, certainly. And like all physical young men I'm sure he's been involved in his share of fights. But as to being a real danger ... no, I don't believe he's capable of that. He's a poseur, likes to show off, talk big. But if the chips were down, I rather suspect he'd turn out a coward.'

I nodded.

'I've heard that opinion before. What about his buddy?'

Abbott looked up. 'You mean the Willis boy, Scott?'

'Yes. The son of the Shelter Cove mayor, I believe. Gus Willis?'

'That's right.' Abbott shook his head. 'Sad case, really. Completely idolizes Bart Anders, follows him around like a poodle. Tries to act tough like he does, but fails miserably. He's an even worse coward than his loud-mouthed friend. Scott Willis is not a bad young man, Mr. Rednapp. Just shallow. Maybe he'll develop yet into someone with backbone and good sense. Let us hope so.' He frowned, leaned forward over the table resting on his arms. 'Why are you so interested in those two? You don't think they had anything to do with Leo's ... accident ... do you?'

'I don't know,' I admitted, after a long silence. 'There are things that might put them in the picture – if the things are true – but as to what actual part they played in Leo Walensky's death, if any, that's still a mystery.'

Abbott sat back.

'I see. Well, I can't imagine what they could have to do with it, but I'm sure you'll find out if there's any connection.' He looked me in the eye and smiled. 'Anything else, Mr. Rednapp?'

I thought about it. Was there anything further this man could tell me that would be useful? For the moment I could think of nothing. If I had missed anything, I could always call him later on.

I drank the last of my coffee, then placed the mug back on the Formica surface.

'No, that's about it, Mr. Abbott. Thanks so much for your time.'

While he finished his coffee, I stepped down to the cash register at one end of the marble counter and paid the bill, leaving a nice tip. When I'd finished Abbot was standing by the door, waiting for me.

Five minutes later I stopped the Cobalt outside his house, leaving the engine idling.

'Thanks again, Mr. Abbott. You've been a great help, and it's been a pleasure meeting you.'

'Likewise, Mr. Rednapp.' He reached across to shake my hand. Then he opened the passenger door and stepped out. 'Don't hesitate to contact me again if you think of anything else that I can do for you.'

'You're very kind, sir.'

Abbott shut the door and I watched him walk up his front path before easing back onto the roadway.

At the end of his street, where it met the main north/south road through the town, I glanced up to my rear-view mirror. A car had turned onto the street behind me and was closing. A small, dark blue car.

An Audi TT convertible.

I pulled onto the main road and headed south, back towards Highway 101.

The convertible had its top up this time and kept well back from me as I moved along the local roads and onto the Highway 101 southbound on-ramp. I couldn't quite see if the driver was alone or if there were two people in the car, but as the mileposts sped by I glanced frequently at the rear-view, keeping an eye on the Audi while maintaining an even 70 mph, right on the speed limit. I was in no hurry, and I wondered what Bart Anders' intention was in shadowing me like this. He made no attempt to overtake, just held to the half-mile or so that separated us. He must have known that I'd noticed him, but he seemed not to care, didn't try to hide behind other vehicles. Maybe that's what he wanted, to hang there like the echo of a bad dream, winding me up.

When I pulled off 101 at the Shelter Cove exit I watched the road behind me. Sure enough, at the requisite half mile the blue car reappeared. On the four-lane the afternoon traffic of cars and vans and eighteen wheelers had been moderate. Here on this road there was hardly any traffic at all. If he wanted to do more than just shadow me from a distance this would be the ideal place for it.

Almost immediately the road started its winding progress through the coastal mountains and I lost sight of him for some minutes. Then I looked up and suddenly saw a dark blue flash behind me as the Audi swept into view and glided up close to my back bumper where it remained, pacing me, only a foot or two away. There were two people in the car; their silhouettes clearly discernible now. The blue Audi hung there behind me for a minute or two in tandem as our two cars swept around corners to the left and then to the right. When a short passing lane suddenly appeared I held in the outside lane and slowed and the blue sports job inched up beside me on the inside, as expected. I glanced towards it. Bart Anders was driving with his faithful poodle Scott in the seat beside him, both boys leering in my direction, taunting me with their eyes. I stared back at them for a moment, then applied the brakes as the passing lane ended, allowing the blue car to shoot ahead of me up the road to disappear around a curve, leaving me alone on the roadway. I breathed a sigh of relief.

Was that to be the end of it?

Five miles further on, just when I had decided they really had given up their game and gone home, I rounded another curve and immediately slammed on the brakes again to avoid rear-ending the Audi as it pootled along before me at a deliberate snail's pace. The road was very twisty here, with no chance for me to swing around them safely, so I was effectively trapped behind them, ambling along through the trees at a sedate, and irritating, 25 mph.

Getting tired of this game, I laid my hand on the horn, gave it two long blasts. There was no change in the Audi's speed. The only reaction was an arm extended from the driver's window flashing me a very distinct middle finger. We wound on through the trees.

After a couple minutes of this the road swept around a curve into what looked to be a half mile long straight stretch – empty of traffic. There was no passing lanes but I could see clearly ahead so, gripping the steering wheel tightly, I swung the car to the left and slammed the accelerator to the floor. The old Cobalt responded magnificently. The sudden maneuver had obviously taken my tormentors by surprise and I had almost passed them before they realized what was happening. Gunning the TT's engine Bart Anders easily pulled abreast again, showing hyena teeth when I glanced quickly in his direction. For a few seconds the cars were neck and neck, racing down the straight stretch together. Then, with only a few hundred yards left ahead before the road turned, I jumped when I saw the bulky snout of a Peterbuilt truck suddenly swing into view – dead ahead of me in my lane and closing fast. Instantly I hit the brakes – only to see that Anders had done the same. The little bastard was trying to hold me in the left lane, preventing me from slipping in behind him! To make matters worse, another car was moving swiftly up behind us, so close now that there was no chance for me to brake suddenly and swing the Cobalt to the right out of the truck's path. Meanwhile the truck continued to race towards me, its bullhorn roaring. There seemed no way out.

And then I saw it.

On the left side of the road ahead was a wide gravel turnout into a state highway department equipment depot.

Braking abruptly I swung the car to the left onto it, just as the Peterbuilt, pulling a high-backed trailer behind it, roared past, its raucous horn echoing through the trees.

Somehow I made it. The car very nearly rolled but I fought it as it switched ends in the gravel before finally coming to rest a foot or two from the lip of a steep-sided drainage ditch. When it stopped I sat stunned for several minutes, waiting for the dust to settle and my heart rate to slow down.

Then I was aware of another car pulling up beside me. I looked out though the dust. It wasn't the Audi. It was the other car that had been behind us – a beat-up silver Mazda. I watched as the driver climbed out and stepped towards me.

'You okay, buddy?' he asked through my window glass, his face twisted with concern.

I rolled the window down.

'Yeah. Thanks.'

'What a bastard,' the man said, glaring off towards the west. 'He wasn't going to let you back in, was he?'

'Seemed that way,' I said. 'Look, thanks a lot for stopping. But I'm fine, the car's fine and the crisis is over. I'll be okay now.'

He looked back at me, frowning.

'You sure? I could call someone on my cell.'

'I've got a cell, too. But there's no need. It's all over. Thanks, though, for your concern. I appreciate it.'

'Okay, buddy. If you say so,' the man said, removing his baseball cap with one hand and scratching his head. 'You take it easy, now.'

'I'll do that.'

He put the cap back on and walked back to his car. Seconds later he had backed around and roared off through the last of the dust towards the coast, leaving me alone to collect myself.

To be honest, it took a little while to do that.

7.

I spent the last few miles of the drive back to Shelter Cove debating whether or not I should call Deputy Williams and put in a formal complaint about Bart Anders' little daredevil ploy. I also wondered whether it had anything to do with the mysterious threatening note I'd found on my car that morning. Finally I decided the whole thing could wait, that there were other more pressing avenues to be explored before I brought to a head my suspicions about that young man and his sidekick. After all he hadn't killed me, and apart from scaring me half to death there'd been no damage caused. But it had been a stupid thing to do, and one that could have turned out quite differently had that turnout not been there. Sooner or later he would hear from me about what I thought of his dangerous little game.

But for the moment I would head back to the motel and give myself an hour's rest before looking up Deputy Williams so that we could compare notes. Not that I expected to learn much from that collation of information. Not yet, anyway. There were still too many holes in the picture, too many vague possibilities. I needed a breakthrough to make it all start to come together.

That breakthrough came a few minutes after I got back to 'The Tides'.

Just as I was about to stretch myself out on the bed for a ten minute power snooze there was a gentle knock on my door. Too faint to be the

96

deputy's. Curious, I stepped across the room and opened it.

Valerie Rush stood on my doorstep, looking nervous.

'Mr. Rednapp,' she began, 'Lee Whipple told me you were staying here. I'm sorry to bother you, but there's something I think you ought to know.'

I considered inviting her inside, then decided that might not look too good to any locals who might be watching and had a better idea.

'Let me grab my jacket. We can walk down to the Cove and I'll treat you to a coffee. How's that strike you?'

'Fine,' she said, smiling. She folded her arms and stood scuffing one of her tennis shoes on the cement walkway while I retrieved my jacket from the back of the armchair and slipped it on. Then, grabbing my notebook from the bedside table, I joined her outside and pulled the door closed behind me.

'Shall we?'

She kept pace with me as we strode out of the motel lot and along the roadside the couple hundred yards to the Cove.

'I hear you're off to San Jose State soon, not too far from my stomping grounds. Is that right?' I asked her as we walked.

'Yes. I've got a part scholarship to study biochemistry there. I'm looking forward to it.'

'I'm sure you'll do fine. I hear San Jose's a good school.'

'It is.'

'You would've been quite close to Leo at Stanford, wouldn't you?'

Her head snapped around to look at me.

'Yes,' she said after a moment, looking forward and down again as we walked. 'We had hoped to see one another regularly.'

There were only a few people in the restaurant so we took my usual booth at the back overlooking the sea. It wasn't Lorraine who served us, but another young lady I hadn't seen before.

'Lorraine not working this afternoon?' I asked her, after we'd ordered our coffees.

She glanced up from her pad.

'She's on her break. Want me to get her?'

'No. I'll see her tonight.'

'Okay.'

She looked me over even more closely when she brought the coffees a little later, then went off smiling. She'd obviously had a word with Lorraine. I was big news.

'Alright, young Val,' I said when the waitress had gone. 'What is it you want to tell me?'

She was clearly uneasy about whatever it was, and sat staring down at the table as she rubbed the back of one hand with the other.

'I wasn't going to tell you because I didn't think it was important. Also I thought you might jump to the wrong conclusion if I did, and I didn't want that.' She sat back, put her hands face down on the banquette on either side of her and met my eyes. 'It's something I saw last week when I went out to Lee's to pick up the broadsheet copies. When I drove past the vista point on my way out there, I saw a car in the parking area, all on its own. I only had a glimpse of it, but I knew who it was. It was Bart's blue Audi. He and Scott Willis were standing in front of it, looking out towards the sea.'

I nodded.

'Interesting. Any idea what they were looking for?'

'Yes. Besides the Cove Restaurant and bar Bart's dad owns another little business down at the harbor – renting boats with outboard motors to tourists for coastal fishing trips. He has two or three of them. Sometimes if the boats are late getting back – I know this from when Bart and I were together – Coach Anders makes him drive up to the vista point to look out for the boats along the shore. Bart keeps a pair of high-powered binoculars in the car to do that with. As you know, you can see a long way up and down the coast from there. Once he sees where the boat is he calls his father on his cell to let him know.'

'And you reckon that was what he was doing when you saw him and Scott Willis at the point that afternoon?'

'I think so. At least, I think I saw Bart holding the binoculars.'

I sat back, putting this piece of information together with the other bits Val had given me the day before at Leland Whipple's. I pulled out my notebook and opened it up to check the details.

'You said yesterday that you met Leo when you were coming back down Lee Whipple's drive after picking up the broadsheets. Is that right?'

'Yes. He was just about to turn into the drive when I got to the road.'

'And you'd been at the Whipples' for only a few minutes?'

She nodded. 'I had to get the car back for Mom.'

I stared at her, thinking.

'What happened then?' I asked. 'When you saw Leo at the bottom of the drive did you stop and have a chat? Or what?'

She looked down again, her nerves obviously returning.

'I stopped. We talked through the car window at first. On my side. Then I got out and gave him a hug.'

I was still staring at her, my mind striving to understand.

'You gave him a hug.'

'Yes.'

'Did you kiss him, Val?' I asked, after a beat.

She glanced up quickly, as if I had somehow caught her out.

'Yes, I did,' she said, after a long pause.

I reached out to put my hand over hers on the table.

'It's all right. I'm not going to tell anybody about it unless I have to. In any case, I don't think it makes any difference now.'

'No,' she murmured. 'I guess it doesn't.'

I sat back again.

'Val, I know you can't see the vista point from Leland Whipple's house, but do you think you could see it from the bottom of his drive, down near the beach?' I asked her.

She frowned. 'I ... I've never noticed.' Then she looked up at me, her eyes widening as she followed my thinking. 'Do you think Bart saw me and Leo together?'

'I don't know.' I leaned forward. 'Was Bart's car still at the vista point when you went back by?'

'No. It'd gone.'

'And you didn't see him again after that?'

'No.'

I wrote down Val's story in the notebook, then closed it, sat back and slipped it into my pocket, reaching for my coffee.

'Thanks for telling me that, Val. It might not mean anything. But it does put Bart Anders and Scott Willis out at the point that afternoon.'

She sat up, looking at me with determination.

'Bart wouldn't have done anything really bad to Leo, Mr. Rednapp. He isn't that kind. I don't want you to think that just because he was out there that he had anything to do with what happened later on.'

'I don't think anything yet, Val. I'm still gathering information. And I assure you I won't think the worst of Bart Anders unless or until there is no other option.'

A part of me wanted to mention my run in with Bart and Scott on the road that afternoon, but I held fire. Valerie seemed disturbed enough as it was.

We made small talk for five or ten more minutes, then I paid for the coffees and walked Valerie back to the motel, where she climbed into her mother's car and drove away. I watched her go, then got into my own car, backed it around and headed out of town toward the road to the vista point.

There was no one there when I arrived – nothing but the long-shadowed afternoon stillness and the sound of distant waves crashing on rocks. I stepped over the railing and moved to stand a few feet from the cliff edge, looking to my right, northwards. The point pushed out from the trees along the roadway, and a good half of the distant beach was in view beside the sea. Just inland from the beach a bit of the road could be seen snaking along parallel with it, until it climbed up the rise beyond. The turning to Leland Whipple's drive was clearly visible.

Had Bart Anders noticed Val's car drive past? I imagined his curiosity as to where she was going. Would he have stepped out here, picked up the car with his binoculars as it came into view on the road below, watched it turn up the Whipple drive?

Val had said she'd stayed only a few minutes at the Whipples', then had returned down the drive – meeting Leo at the bottom. They had talked. She had got out, hugged him. And then kissed him.

Had Bart Anders seen that, too?

But Val had also said the vista point car park was empty when she drove back past it.

When had Bart Anders gone?

More importantly, had he come back – when Leo Walensky was making his return journey past the vista point?

That was the question to which I was dying to know the answer.

It had been a few hours since my lunch with Guy Abbott and I was starting to feel a little hungry so I stopped at the general store and went in to pick up something light to tide me over until dinner. Behind the counter was a hot dog grill, with dogs and buns stacked and ready to serve in a warmer at one side. I ordered a foot-long with relish and mustard and grabbed a can of Diet Pepsi to have with it. Then I took my purchases outside to sit at a picnic bench at the side of the store. While I ate my dog cars came and went. A sea breeze rustled the tree branches nearby. The store, as usual, was pretty busy.

I was just finishing off the last bite when I glanced up to see a man striding towards me across the parking lot. He was wearing a high church dog collar under his jacket, and a cloth cap, and he was frowning. Remembering my first conversation with Lorraine, I had a pretty good idea who he was without him telling me. In any case I'd seen him the day before, chatting with some of his flock on the church steps.

'I believe you are Mr. Rednapp,' he said when he arrived,

glowering down at me. 'The reporter looking into the death of the Walensky boy. Am I right?'

I wiped my mouth with the paper napkin, balled that and the hotdog wrapper into my fist and stood to drop the lot into the garbage can at the side of the store. Then I turned back to him, wiping my hands together.

'You're right,' I told him. 'What can I do for you, Reverend Baker?'

He didn't seem surprised that I knew who he was. He looked around to see if anyone was watching, then leaned toward me.

'Mind if I sit with you for a bit? I'd like to have a talk with you.'

'Help yourself,' I said, gesturing towards the bench.

Taking off his cap, he sat on one side of the table, I on the other. Leaning forward he clasped his hands together, clutching the crumpled cap, almost as if praying.

'I heard you've been talking to people about that boy and I wanted to let you know my own thoughts about all this.'

I nodded.

'I'm listening.'

Baker frowned.

'The fact is that Walensky boy was a bad seed. Not only had he rejected belief in God himself, he also made it his business to try to turn other people along his same deluded path. I think he must have been a little ... mentally unwell, to put it bluntly.'

'Did you know the boy, Reverend Baker?'

'Only by sight. Obviously he never came to church. And his parents, though apparently believers, are not Episcopalians.'

'So if you didn't know Leo Walensky, sir, based upon what evidence do you make these allegations against him?'

Baker's face clouded even further.

'A lot of my parishioners have complained to me about him. They knew it was him that put those heathen broadsheets in our mailboxes. They were upset and they asked me to do what I could to stop him. I went to his parents, tried to reason with them. But they just ignored me, let the boy go on doing what he wanted.'

I shrugged. 'He wasn't breaking any laws by distributing those broadsheets, Reverend Baker.'

'No, but he was offending the community, talking blasphemy. There should be laws against such things, but unfortunately there aren't any. Yet.'

'I see. What about good old American 'freedom of speech', Reverend? Isn't that all Leo Walensky was exercising? After all, there was no kind of coercion involved. All people had to do was to ignore the broadsheets and throw them away.'

Baker bristled.

'You're not getting the point, Rednapp.'

'Oh? And what is the point, sir?'

'That boy was not right in his head. He had crazy ideas and lived off in his own private world. It's well known he had no friends. God alone knows what kind of deviant thoughts ran rampant through his mind. All I'm saying – and the reason I wanted to talk to you about him – is that there's no reason to doubt that he took his own life out there at that vista point. He was unbalanced, clearly unstable. And his radical ideas finally drove him over the edge – literally.'

'You believe Leo Walensky took his own life?'

''Course I do. Driven to it, probably, by guilty voices in his head. He wasn't a normal boy, Mr. Rednapp. No normal boy thinks and believes as he does. Did.'

I stood up. I'd had enough.

'Thanks for sharing your thoughts, Reverend. I'll bear them in mind.'

'You'd better,' the man said, getting up himself. 'There's no point in you digging around here anymore, bothering people with your questions. This town suffered enough from the doings of that boy while he was alive. They shouldn't have to go on suffering because of him now that he's gone.'

And fixing the cap on his head again he turned and strode away.

I watched him go, then drained the last of my Diet Pepsi, dropped the can in the recycling bin, and headed for my car.

Deputy Horace Williams was waiting for me at the motel when I pulled in. He was sitting in his 4 X 4 outside my room with his driver's door open, reading a copy of the *Humboldt Times* and nursing a coffee in a Styrofoam cup. As I climbed out of the Cobalt he did the same from his vehicle and we met at my door, he carrying his coffee.

'Convenient time?' he asked as I approached.

'Couldn't be more so,' I said.

I unlocked the door and beckoned him inside. He stepped in before me and moved immediately to the armchair, lowering himself into it and placing the cup on the low table beside it. I shut the front door behind me and moved over to drop my jacket on the bed, taking my former position sitting at its foot.

'So,' I said, producing my notebook and pen. 'Any news?'

Williams sat back in his chair.

'Well, since I saw you yesterday I've had the forensics report on the DNA test they ran on the bloody fingerprint on that broadsheet – comparing it with Leo Walensky's DNA.'

'And?'

'It's the same. That's definitely Leo's blood in that fingerprint.'

I nodded. 'I suppose the print itself was too messy to determine whose finger it was that made it?'

'No chance. There wasn't enough detail. But at least we now know that Leo was bleeding before he fell from that cliff. What about you?' he concluded. 'You come up with anything sensational since yesterday?'

I dug into my jacket pocket for the threatening note and handed it across to him. He opened it out and read the message.

'I found that stuck under my wiper blade this morning.'

Frowning, Williams refolded the note and sat back.

'Mind if I keep it?' he asked.

'Not at all. I thought you'd want to.'

He stuck it into his shirt pocket.

'Could've just been someone horsing around. Any idea who sent it?'

'Maybe. But there's more. I also found a witness that puts Bart Anders and Scott Willis out at that vista point an hour or two before Leo Walensky died there.'

The deputy leaned forward, frowning.

'Bart Anders?'

'And his sidekick, yes.'

'Who's your witness?'

I spent the next half hour bringing the red-haired deputy up to speed on all of my interviews over the preceding thirty-six hours, and the bits of new information each had provided – including Val's confession about the kiss (with a request for him to keep that to himself for the moment). I didn't offer any conclusions as to what all these clues added up to because I wasn't sure of that yet myself. I finished off with an account of my run in with Bart Anders' blue Audi on the way back from Fortuna, and described in detail the danger I had faced because of it. When I finished speaking, Deputy Williams sat back on the armchair and shook his head, frowning.

'That's hard to believe,' he said at last. 'I've known Bart since he was small. Oh, he's a bit of a show-off and a braggart, throws his weight around sometimes, but I've never known him to do anything downright evil.' He stopped, frowning. 'Still, that business on the road sounds pretty evil, whether or not he intended it that way.'

'I rather suspect he didn't,' I returned. 'I had a last glimpse of his face while the truck was bearing down on me before I swung left onto the turnout. His eyes were as big as saucers with shock and surprise. That must've been when he realized I couldn't simply brake and slip in behind him because the other car had come up too fast behind. I don't think he intended for me to get creamed by that truck. I think he just wanted to throw a scare into me, put me off doing any more investigating.'

'You think he might also have left that note for you?'

I shrugged. 'It's possible.'

Williams reached for his coffee, took a sip, then leaned forward in the chair again, cradling the cup in his two hands.

'So you think Bart Anders – who's obviously still sweet on the Rush girl – saw her and the Walensky boy kissing and then came back later and did him in?'

I shook my head.

'No. That's too pat. Anyway everyone tells me Bart Anders isn't that kind of guy, even if he does have a temper.'

'So what do you think happened?'

'I've no idea. I think it did have to do with Anders seeing Val and Leo kissing, but what actually happened out at the vista point later is still a total mystery to me.'

Williams nodded slowly, thinking.

'Sounds like we need to talk to Bart and young Scott,' he said at last.

'I think that'd be a good idea,' I said. 'But I want both the boys' fathers there, too, during the interview.'

'They'd have to be there anyway,' Williams said. 'Or an attorney representing them.'

'Let's keep it informal at this stage,' I urged him. 'We're not absolutely sure there was any skullduggery committed out on that point and I don't want to come down on them with all guns blazing at the start. Let's see what we can draw out of them by being nice and gentle, shall we? At least, at first?'

'Sounds like a plan.' He finished his coffee, dropped the empty cup into the wastebasket beside the table. 'When you want to do this? Tonight?'

'No,' I told him. 'I want some time to put all these things together in my mind before we question them. How about tomorrow afternoon?'

Williams nodded.

'I'll set it up.' He got to his feet, sighing deeply. 'Hell. It begins to look like we're going to have to reopen that case after all.' He grinned sheepishly. 'Sheriff Dunlap won't like it.'

'It's not your fault, Deputy. All this came to light after your initial investigation.'

I stood and stepped towards him, ready to see him out.

'I think it's time we got to first names,' he said, sticking out a hand. 'I'm known by my friends as "Red".'

I grasped his hand and shook it.

'And I'm Arnie.' He stood waiting while I opened the door for him. 'You'll let me know when and where tomorrow?'

'I will. Probably leave word here. Or with Lorraine.' He grinned. 'You've landed on your feet there, pardner. She's a great gal.'

I shook my head, smiling.

'There's no keeping secrets in this town, is there?'

'Not hardly,' he said, stepping out the door. 'You take care now, Arnie.'

'You, too, Red.'

I watched him climb into his rig and pull out of the motel lot and onto the road.

Then I closed the door again.

I had just showered and was shaving before the bathroom mirror when I heard my cell tinkle in my jacket pocket. I was pretty sure it was Abe Rawlings phoning.

It was.

'What you got to tell me, Arnie?' he said when I answered. 'Is there a story or not?'

'There'll be a story of some kind, to be sure,' I told him. 'But as to what, I'm still in the dark about that. I'll know more tomorrow. I'm having a meeting with some people then that will hopefully blow the whole thing wide open.'

'Good,' he said. 'Because I need you back here soon as you can make it. I'm hearing reports of a possible scandal involving backhanders from the contractors doing the recycling collections for the city. Want you to look into that for me.'

'Fair enough. But I'd like to put this one to bed before I start anything new, Abe. I feel close to wrapping it up, and I could well do that tomorrow.'

'Good luck with it, then,' he said. 'Keep in touch.'

He hung up.

8.

'It really might have been an accident, you know?'

'Hmm? What could've been an accident?'

'Arnie!'

In the darkness Lorraine gently slapped my bare chest with the flat of her hand. I had been on the edge of drifting off into an exhausted, blissful sleep, but that apparently was to be postponed for a few minutes longer.

'Leo Walensky's death, silly,' she said, nuzzling closer into my arm, her cheek resting on my shoulder. 'I've been thinking. It could just have been a tragic accident after all – even if those other boys were involved.'

I fought to clear my head.

'How do you mean?' I asked finally. 'What makes you say that?'

Lorraine and I had spent the evening together as planned – me picking her up from her house and driving the both of us in to Fortuna to enjoy a superb prime rib dinner at the best restaurant the town had to offer. Then we'd come back to her place for an hour of quiet chat and a couple glasses of wine before retiring to bed. We had talked of many things: about my divorce, my daughter Lisa, my work. She told me about her three years spent in Shelter Cove, of trying to come to terms with the end of her own marriage, of the continual unsubtle approaches of her boss, Coach Dale Anders, who had been pressuring her to go out with him ever since his wife had left him eighteen months before. Lorraine had put him off for two reasons, she told me: one, that she was not yet ready to enter into another relationship; and two, that on principle she never mixed her working and personal lives. Smart girl. She also admitted that she found Anders not in the least attractive, and decidedly not her type. Anders, however, apparently found it hard to throw in the towel.

Also, of course, we had talked about Leo Walensky's death and how it might have come about. As I had come to trust her I told Lorraine virtually everything I'd discovered, except the bit about finding the threatening note that morning. I thought that might freak her out. I even dared to run past her a few of my theories as to what might or might not have happened out at the point – always involving, since there didn't seem any other alternative, young Bart Anders and his poodle, Scott Willis. She had listened carefully to what I had to say, then shook her head, frowning slightly.

'I can't believe Bart would do anything deliberately to hurt Leo Walensky, Arnie. Whatever the provocation,' she had said. 'I've seen him a lot in the restaurant, and though he's an arrogant braggart like his father, and has surely missed the calming influence of his mother these past months, he's basically not a bad kid. Just headstrong and full of himself. No,' she finished, 'he's no murderer, sweetheart. I'm sure of that.'

I had considered her remarks carefully, and had decided to keep an open mind about Bart Anders when I met him the next day, given the marginally positive accounts I'd received about him from seemingly reliable people.

'What makes you think that?' I said again now, squeezing her arm gently. 'That it could've been just an accident after all?'

'Mmm,' she said. 'I'm just thinking that maybe Bart and Scott did set off to intimidate Leo to start with, to scare him off seeing the Rush girl, and it all went horribly wrong somehow. Couldn't they have been caught up in a situation that, well, just got out of control?

Leo's death might've been just a tragic accident.'

I gave the idea some thought.

'I guess it's possible. But there are still some pretty suspicious facts about the case – facts that tend to suggest another scenario altogether. The glasses, for instance, apparently thrown off to one side. The balled-up broadsheet I found at the vista point with Leo's blood on it. The way the bicycle had apparently been tossed into the bushes. And finally, the very fact of Leo's falling from the cliff edge at all – or being thrown off. No, I don't think I can accept the accident story without knowing exactly what happened out there. And I'm hoping Deputy Williams and I can bring that out into the open at our interview with the boys tomorrow.'

'Well,' Lorraine said, running her fingers through my chest hair. 'Just don't go there having made up your mind those boys are guilty of murder. Wait till you know what really happened.'

'Thanks for the good advice, boss.' I turned to plant a kiss on her warm forehead. 'That's exactly what I intend to do.'

I was going through my notes again in my room at the motel late the following morning, after having taken my run and breakfasted at the Cove, when the phone beside my bed rang. It was Red Williams.

'Morning, pardner,' he opened.

'Morning yourself, Deputy. What's the word?'

'Dale Anders will have his son and Gus and Scott Willis together at his place at two o'clock this afternoon. Just after lunch. That all right for you?'

'Perfect. How did Anders react when you asked for the meeting?' Red Williams chuckled.

'Well, he didn't sound happy. But he reckons the only way we can put this whole thing to bed is to have it out once and for all, so he's resigned to doing that. I don't think he imagines for a moment there's any connection between those boys and what happened out at the point.'

'No, I'm sure he doesn't.'

'Want me to pick you up?'

'Might be easier. You know where he lives. What time?'

'It's not far from you. I'll drop by at one-fifty. All right?'

'Sounds good. See you then.'

We hung up.

The Anders house was probably the biggest of the new ranch-style homes in Shelter Cove, and it sat back from the town on a slight rise at one end of the peninsula, overlooking a broad, immaculately kept lawn and the flat blue sea.

Dale Anders met us at the door, his face a mask of perturbation and distaste. He mumbled a perfunctory greeting, then opened the door wide and ushered us into the house, leading us along a corridor past a spacious living room, dining room and kitchen area and into a glass-roofed den at the back of the house. The den was huge, with a giant flat-screen television on one wall, three-foot high speakers in all four corners, and an assortment of leather divans, armchairs and recliners spread around on all sides. Brightly colored rugs were thrown here and there over the tiled floor. Through the sliding doors and floor to ceiling windows beyond I could see a swimming pool, surrounded by a concrete walkway and a six-foot high redwood fence holding back the encircling evergreens.

Mayor Gus Willis and his son Scott were seated on one of the dark leather sectionals at the right of the room. Bart Anders was standing behind the bar at the left of the entrance door, filling a tall glass from a soft drink can. Coach Anders stepped forward to the middle of the room and turned, swinging an arm in a wide gesture.

'Have a seat, gentlemen.'

Williams and I sat on either end of a light-colored leather divan positioned at the back center of the room. Bart Anders carried his glass from the bar and sat with his father to the left of us, both in heavy upholstered recliner armchairs facing the television screen across the room.

'Now then, Red,' Anders said, when he was seated and comfortable. 'I can cut this whole thing short by telling you that Bart has confessed to me what happened out on the highway yesterday, that he and Scott did a crazy-ass thing driving like fools trying to throw a scare into Mr. Rednapp there, just for fun, like, and that it all went pear-shaped on them.' Smirking, he produced a check book from a pocket. 'They're both real sorry, so if that's why you're here I'm willing to make amends to Mr. Rednapp by ...'

'Hold on a minute, Dale,' the deputy interrupted, raising a hand. He looked from Anders to me and then back again. 'I know about all that, and it sounds serious enough in itself. We'll talk about that later. But the fact is that ain't why we're here.'

'Oh?' said the coach, sitting back with a puzzled expression. 'Then what's this all about?'

Red Williams leaned forward, resting his elbows on his knees. 'As you know, Dale, Mr. Rednapp has been asking around about the death of young Leo Walensky and, well, he's come up with some pieces of evidence that suggest the boy didn't just die from a simple accident or suicide out there like we thought.'

Anders' eyebrows rose.

'Really? What kind of ... evidence?'

'Well, for one thing there's the question of the boy's glasses and where they were found. Leo Walensky had to wear those glasses in bright sunlight, we all know that. While he may have taken them off to clean them or whatever, there's no reason they should've been tossed off to the side of the parking area onto the rough ground. That makes no sense. So someone must have done that for him.'

Anders straightened.

'Someone?'

'That's right,' I said, entering the conversation. 'It's almost certain Leo Walensky was not alone at the point when he died.'

'How do you know that?' Anders asked after a moment, frowning. 'And who could it possibly have been?'

'We'll get to that in a minute.' I turned to Red. 'Deputy Williams, maybe you can tell them about what I found out there the day I got here, and what it represents?'

Red Williams sat back and cleared his throat. Then he reached into an inside pocket and produced a folded copy of the broadsheet I'd found crumpled up in the bushes at the vista point, with its red fingerprint on one edge. He stood, crossed the room, and handed it to Anders, who took it and looked it over.

'What's this?' Anders asked finally.

'A color photocopy of one of Leo Walensky's broadsheets,' Red told him. 'You can see the date at the top, Dale. It was last week's issue.' He turned back towards me. 'Mr. Rednapp found the original of that sheet balled up in a bush out at the vista point and gave it to me the day he got here – last Friday. As you probably know, the rest of the broadsheets weren't delivered around town until Sunday night, two nights ago – several days after the boy's death. Now leaving aside for a minute the question of who it was that delivered the broadsheets,' and here Red looked at me with raised eyebrows, 'the fact remains that this one was found out there at the point beforehand, and that almost certainly means that Leo had the copy on him when he got there that day.'

'How can you know that?' scoffed Gus Willis in a reedy voice. It was the first time I'd ever heard him speak. 'That could've been dropped by anyone out there on that day, or before, and at any time. There's no reason necessarily to believe that the Walensky boy was carrying it. Besides,' he said, sitting back, 'what the hell difference does it make who dropped the damned thing out there? What can it possibly have to do with the boy's death anyhow?'

Red looked from Willis back to Coach Anders.

'Dale, you see that red smudge on the edge of the broadsheet?'

Anders peered down at the sheet.

'Yeah. What about it?'

'Well, that's a bloody fingerprint. I had a DNA test done on the original. The blood belongs to Leo Walensky.'

I was watching the two boys, whose eyes were riveted on the broadsheet copy. Bart Anders' face was set in a slight frown, his eyes glaring. Scott Willis, on the other hand, had sat back in his seat with his hands clasped tightly in his lap. He looked like he'd just seen a ghost. It was clear they both knew exactly what the broadsheet was and what it meant.

Coach Anders looked up, puzzled now.

'How could Leo Walensky's blood have gotten on there? What does this mean?'

I stood up, walked across the room to stand beside Red, looking down at the coach.

'It means that Leo had been bloodied up before he landed on those rocks at the foot of the cliff. It probably means ...' and here I deliberately glanced across at Bart Anders. 'It probably means,' I repeated, 'that somebody *caused* Leo to bleed up there, by striking him or causing him to fall or somehow otherwise to injure himself.'

Both boys remained frozen in their seats, their eyes locked on mine. I turned back to Coach Anders.

'What're you driving at, Rednapp?' he asked, his eyes narrowing. 'You're not suggesting that my boy ... our boys ... had anything to do with this, are you? Because if you are ...'

'Dale,' Red Williams interrupted, pulling another folded paper from his pocket. 'Mr. Rednapp found this stuck under one of his wiper blades this morning at the motel.'

He handed the paper to the Coach, who unfolded and read it, frowning. Then he refolded it and handed it back to the Deputy.

'Surely that's just somebody's idea of a practical joke,' he scoffed. 'I guess Mr. Rednapp must've got a few people riled up with all his poking around.'

'Dale,' Red Williams said, ignoring him, 'did you send Bart and

Scott up to the point that afternoon to look out for one of your boats?'

Anders sat back, suddenly silent, blinking. He glanced at his son, then back at the deputy.

'I may have done. What's that got to do with anything?'

'Maybe nothing,' I said, returning to the divan and sitting again. 'But if you did it puts them out at the point at a time when they might have witnessed certain events that were taking place near there – events they might not have been too happy about.'

'What events?' Gus Willis asked, frowning now.

I turned to the boys; first Bart, then his friend.

'You boys want to say anything here?' I asked. 'You know this story better than I do.'

Bart Anders scowled.

'You're crazy,' he growled. 'I know nothing and I got nothing to say.'

I stared at him.

'You deny you were up on the point that afternoon?'

He shifted on his chair.

'Hell no, I don't deny it. Dad told me to go up there to look for a boat and I went, and Scott went with me. I looked out from the point and saw it. Then I called Dad on my cell and told him it was coming in. And that was that.'

'Then you came back to town?' Red asked, having retrieved the broadsheet copy from Anders and taking it across now to Gus Willis for him to examine. 'Is that right?'

'Yessir,' Bart said.

Red looked at him.

'And you didn't see anything up there?'

'No,' Bart said, a little too forcefully. 'We didn't see nothing but that boat.'

The deputy turned to the mayor's son.

'That so, Scott?'

'What?' the boy returned, glancing up nervously from the

broadsheet copy, as if distracted from other thoughts. 'Is what so, sir?'

Red sighed.

'Bart says you boys went up there, saw the boat Dale had asked him to look for, phoned him the news, and then came back to town. He says you saw nothing while you were up there apart from the boat. Is that the truth?'

Scott Willis couldn't prevent a quick glance to his friend, who stared back at him.

'Y-yes. It's true. All of it. We didn't see anything or anyone up there.'

'No one at all? No other cars? Nothing?'

'Nothing,' the boy said, almost a whisper. 'We didn't see anything up there.'

Gus Willis could tell something was not right about that reply. He glanced up from the broadsheet copy to his son's face, frowning.

'Scott! Is that the truth?'

'Yes, Dad.'

'You didn't see anything at all up there other than that boat?'

'No, sir. We looked for that boat, and when Bart saw it coming in we phoned the coach and then we came back.'

I shook my head, sadly. Red Williams took the broadsheet from the mayor and brought it back to the divan to sit next to me. He folded the sheet and put it and the threatening note back into his inside pocket and for a long moment no one said anything and the silence hung in the room like a bad smell. Finally I sat forward.

'There's something else,' I said, to everyone in general. 'Valerie Rush told me she drove out that way around 4 PM that afternoon. She was on her way to visit the Whipples. She says that when she passed the vista point she saw Bart's blue Audi parked there, saw Bart and Scott out on the point. She said she thought Bart was using the binoculars.'

'There!' Bart barked. 'You see? I said that's all we did out there.'

'And you didn't notice Valerie's mother's car go past with Val herself driving?'

'No I didn't,' he returned, smirking. 'I was looking out to sea with the binoculars, wasn't I?'

I turned to the other boy.

'What about you, Scott? You weren't looking out to sea all the time, were you? Did you notice Val pass on the road and tell Bart about it? And did he then wait till she came into view on the road below and watch her with the glasses till she turned up the Whipple's drive?'

The boy said nothing, though his eyes spoke volumes.

'And then a little later did you see Leo Walensky pass the vista point on his bicycle and tell Bart about that, too? You did, didn't you? And then Bart watched the beach road with his glasses again, didn't he? And saw Leo Walensky arrive at the Whipple's drive just as Val was coming back out of it, isn't that so? And they both stopped and talked together for a bit, didn't they? Talked and ... and then hugged. And Bart saw all of that, didn't he, Scott? Isn't that what happened? Hm? You can tell the truth, son. There's nothing to be afraid of.'

Scott's eyes roamed from mine to the deputy's, then to his father's, then to Bart's and Dale Anders' and back to mine again. But he said nothing.

'Come on, Scott,' his father urged, darkly. 'Say something. Don't just sit there like a bump on a log. Did you or did you not see anything out there at the point that afternoon? Spit it out, boy!'

For a long moment Scott's eyes blinked like he was having difficulty focusing and his breath seemed to come in gasps. Then he sat forward, his hands on his thighs. His voice when it came was a high-pitched squeal.

'Yes!' he said at last, in a rush. 'I saw the car! I told Bart it was Val! I ...'

'SHUT UP!' Bart roared, jumping to his feet. 'You shut your goddam mouth, Scott!'

'Bart, we ...'

'I said SHUT IT!'

Bart stepped toward Scott, glaring.

Coach Anders' face tightened and he rose up from his chair. For a long moment he stared at his son, shocked and angry. When he spoke, it was in a low command.

'Sit down, Bart.'

Bart Anders stopped staring at his friend and turned to face his father.

'Dad, I...'

'I said sit down!'

Bart blinked at his father for some seconds. Then he moved to settle again onto his chair, sitting back, a look of resigned submission on his face.

'Now then,' the coach said, stepping forward with hands on hips and positioning himself to glare at both of the youngsters in turn. 'I think it's time we hear the truth, boys. No more shilly-shallying. No more bluster. I want you both to own up to what happened up there – even if it's bad. I want you to be men. You hear me?' When neither boy spoke, he stepped towards his son, narrowing his eyes. 'Bart, I said did you hear me?'

'Yes, Dad.'

'Then talk!'

No cockiness in his son now. Just shame.

And guilt.

And after a moment they did talk. First one, and then the other.

And the story came out, bit by bit, until all the facts were finally clear.

Lorraine had been right. It had been an accident. A stupid bit of farcical play-acting that had gone too far and ended in tragedy.

Scott Willis had indeed seen Valerie Rush drive by in her mother's car, and had told Bart about it. With his binoculars Bart had watched the car reappear on the road below, had seen it turn up the drive to the Whipple place. Curious, he had remained a few minutes to see what would happen next. The first thing that happened was that Leo Walensky had passed the vista point on his bicycle, heading the same direction Valerie had gone. Bart had trained the glasses down again on Leo's figure when it appeared pedaling along on the road below, followed it as it moved towards the Whipple driveway, saw him arrive there just as Val's car reappeared at the end of it. The binoculars made it all seem so close. Bart had watched them talk. Watched Valerie climb out of the car, smiling, to hug Leo.

Watched her kiss him.

Furious, Bart had climbed into the Audi with Scott and driven back to town, determined to teach Leo Walensky a lesson at the first opportunity. No half-blind weirdo was going to move in on his girl. Bart would give him a fright he would not forget, and that'd be the end of it. Val would see reason. Eventually he would win her back. He had to win her back. He loved her.

Back at the cove, Bart and Scott had closed up the boat rental office. Then they'd gone back to the point for a smoke before they headed off to their separate homes. Standing out on the point again, watching the sunset build, they had seen Leo Walensky reappear from the Whipple's driveway on his bicycle and start up the road towards them. Bart Anders had smiled. An opportunity for him to effect his plan of intimidation had just been dropped providentially into his lap.

When Leo reached the vista point turnout they were waiting for him. Leo had tried to get by them, but Bart had pulled him off the bike onto the asphalt, then thrown the bike off into the bushes at the roadside. Leo had regained his feet and a push and shove contest had ensued – Bart forcing Leo continually back with shoves to his chest while telling him in no uncertain terms what dire consequences awaited him if he didn't leave Valerie Rush alone, that she was Bart's girl, and that Leo would be suffering from more than just bad eyes if he kept up his friendship with her. Leo Walensky, unwilling to be drawn into a fight, had merely tried to fend him off. Until Bart had said something that Leo simply couldn't tolerate – had called him a 'four-eyed Polack faggot', or some similar insult to his affliction, his parentage and his sexuality, and Leo had lost his cool. In a sudden rage, Leo had hurled himself back at Bart, and Bart, surprised, had struggled with him, at one point pulling off Leo's glasses by the elastic strap and hurling them off to the side in an effort to get the boy to stop attacking him. And when that hadn't done the trick, when Leo had continued to press forward, pounding with closed fists on Bart's head and shoulders and arms, Scott Willis – who up to now had only stood back watching and catcalling – had lunged forward. Grabbing one of Leo's flailing arms, he'd swung the boy around at arm's length in a wide circle, loosing him finally to sail off-balance across the pavement beside the blue Audi to fall heavily onto his back on the rocky verge just inside the steel safety rail – Leo's head unfortunately crashing back sharply onto a jutting spike of rock near the rail that had crushed the back of his head like a hammer into a ripe pear. Leo had died instantly. When the boys saw he wasn't moving, and realized that he wasn't going to move again – saw the thick, dark blood that was oozing from his broken skull – they panicked. What to do with a dead boy? They had to move fast before someone came along.

It was Bart's idea to toss him from the cliff, to make it look as if he'd either fallen by accident or taken his own life.

As they pulled the body over the railing, the zip on Leo's rucksack had opened slightly and they'd seen the broadsheet pages within. Scott had plunged a hand inside to pluck one out, thereby planting a bloody fingerprint on it. When he saw the blood, he crumpled the sheet and tossed it – not out over the cliff as he ought to have done, but unthinkingly back towards the brush at the side. The breeze had sailed it further along, to where it had caught in the bush to be found by me three days later. The rucksack and other broadsheet copies they had taken away with them, burying the lot in the woods behind Bart's house that evening. They had found Leo's cell phone, too, in the rucksack. That they had switched off and tossed as far as they could from the cliff top into the sea. Then they had used a bottle of drinking water to wash away the blood on the rocks and their hands, and had gone home. Hoping against hope that the suicide/accident story would mask their guilt once Leo's body had been found.

It almost had.

If I hadn't come along to poke my nose into things – if Abe Rawlings hadn't smelled a rat and sent me to Shelter Cove to investigate what had really happened to his nephew – they would almost certainly have gotten away with it.

Epilogue

'What will happen to them?' Lorraine asked, after sipping at her gin and tonic. 'The boys, I mean. Will they spend a long time in jail?'

We were sitting on the deck at the back of Deputy Williams' house – Lorraine and I and Red and his wife, Edna. It was several days later and Lorraine's daughter Mandy – now returned from the visit with her father – sat on the deck floor a few feet from us, trying to entertain Red's two-year-old daughter by carefully constructing teetering piles of wooden building blocks for the little one to knock down. Edna Williams sat beside her husband, bottle-feeding their baby son.

Red Williams leaned forward from his chair, a half-full beer bottle in one hand.

'Well, it kinda depends on how sorry the jury thinks they are at the trial,' he told Lorraine, answering her question. 'If they show real remorse, and their fathers offer some kind of financial restitution to the Walenskys for their suffering, then the jury might ask the judge to be lenient in his sentencing. If that's the case they could get off with only a year or two inside, with a suspended sentence on top of that to keep them on the straight and narrow.'

'I don't think the jury will have any trouble deciding Leo's death was an accident,' I said in turn. 'So the worst the boys will face is a charge of manslaughter. It'll also count in their favor that both of them are young, and that neither has ever been in trouble before. But the most important thing, I agree with Red, is whether or not they can convince the jury they're genuinely sorry for what happened. I think they'll do that, because I think they are both sorry. And ashamed.'

It was the Saturday after Leo Walensky's funeral and I had stayed on – with Abe Rawlings' blessing – to spend the weekend in Shelter Cove before heading back to take up my new assignment at the *Bulletin* on the Monday. My article on Leo's death had appeared in the paper on Friday, and so it was now just a matter of wrapping things up – of saying goodbyes and offering thanks for the help I had had along the way. I was also, I had to admit, pleased to be spending a bit more time with Lorraine and her gawky but loveable daughter, to both of whom I was growing increasingly attached. An on-going long distance relationship between us now seemed very likely, and while it did mean frequent long drives up and down highway 101 at weekends, the pleasure of spending time with them in such peaceful, relaxed surroundings would be compensation enough.

After the boys had made their full confession Red had telephoned the Sheriff's office in Eureka and had a car sent down to take them up to the county seat for booking. The charge at that point was simply perverting the course of justice, but a further charge of manslaughter or some-such was possibly pending. The boys had spent a sobering night in the Eureka jail, until bail had been posted for each by their wealthy fathers and they were allowed to come home to await the trial. That would take place in just over two months. For the moment they were allowed to continue with their plans for college – in the hope that their sentencing would allow them to attend as soon as was possible. Given their social position and previously clean records it seemed likely that whatever the sentence they would not be kept too long from pursuing their further education.

When we'd left the Anders' house that afternoon, Red and I had stopped by the Walenskys' to tell Leo's parents the truth about what had happened to their son. They'd taken it in good part, though Connie Walensky could not suppress a growl about how he'd always known

Bart Anders was a no-good bully. The reports by both Red and I of Bart's tearful confession, however, eventually brought Leo's father back to a more sanguine state of acceptance, if not forgiveness. For clearly, in spite of the boys' malevolent intentions that afternoon, what had happened had been a complete shock to both of them. And, given their youth, they might even perhaps be forgiven for their panicky and short-sighted decision to hide the truth of what had happened by faking the accident/suicide. It would be the jury's and the court's job to work out the right degree of punishment for that lapse of judgement. Whatever the result, it hopefully would provide a stark lesson for the boys that would temper their behavior for the rest of their lives.

Leo's funeral had been a quiet affair, held at his mother's Quaker Meeting House in Fortuna. Among the two dozen or so attendees were several familiar faces: Lee and Ang Whipple, Leo's old Shelter Cove Principal Hazel Mendoza, kindly Gus Abbott, looking deeply sad in his rumpled tweed jacket and bow tie. And Valerie Rush and her parents. I even noticed Deputy Red Williams sitting quietly in a back row. In deference to Leo's beliefs – or, to be precise, non-beliefs – no reference was made during the short service to God or to an afterlife, and it ended with a simply voiced wish that Leo's spirit might be received well by whatever benevolent governing force existed out there in the void. That was considered sufficient by all present to give the youthful atheist a proper and respectful send-off.

Abe Rawlings had driven up from the Bay area with his wife, and had sat at the front of the service with his sister Muriel and her husband and daughter and the rest of their extended families. I had sat with Lorraine towards the back. When the service concluded we joined the others at the little crematorium at the edge of town where Leo's remains were committed to their final fiery end.

All in all it was a tasteful and very moving ceremony, and even though I had not known Leo Walensky personally I was glad to have been able to attend the ritual marking his passing, to have been able to pay my silent respects to a young man who had dared to be different, who had believed that there must be another way for humankind than the path that has led to so much suffering and hatred and despair.

And who, in a small way, had tried to do something about it.

Had he lived Leo Walensky would almost certainly have continued striving for a world that was more tolerant towards new ideas, more open to challenging the old shibboleths of blind faith, tradition and superficial honor, more devoted to righting the world's wrongs through the application of mankind's innate capacity for reason, compassion and understanding rather than relying on 'divine' intervention. I cannot help but believe that such an influence would have made his homeland a marginally better place. We shall miss his contribution – perhaps the flutter of the butterfly's wing that could eventually have changed the world. And I shall long remember his loss, even though I never knew him.

It would, I think, behoove us all to do so.

About the Author

(Photo by Bob Bailey)

William Roberts is an American actor, writer and voice artist resident in the UK for over forty years. Born in Oregon, he was raised and educated in northern California, and still proudly carries a US passport. He currently lives and works in London, enjoying his writing, flying his small airplane around Europe and watching his grandsons grow.

Also by WERoberts

An Ill Wind

After witnessing the recovery of a mysterious mutilated body in a public park in Northern California, San Francisco reporter Arnold Rednapp becomes embroiled in an investigation involving drugs, gangs, pedophilia, political corruption and murder, and follows a trail of clues that extends the full length of California and deep into Mexico. As he closes in on the villains, their desperate efforts to avoid capture result in a climactic finale that brings the lives of Arnie and several of his closest friends to within a whisker of extinction.

A tense thriller, filled with memorable characters and plot twists, that moves inexorably toward its breathtaking finish.

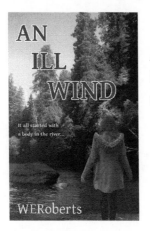

Available on Amazon as a quality paperback, in Kindle format, and soon as a downloadable audiobook read by the author.

Printed in Great Britain
by Amazon